CRITICAL PERSPECTIVES ON
MINORS PLAYING
HIGH-CONTACT
SPORTS

ANALYZING THE ISSUES

CRITICAL PERSPECTIVES ON
MINORS PLAYING HIGH-CONTACT SPORTS

Edited by John A. Torres

Published in 2017 by Enslow Publishing, LLC
101 W. 23rd Street, Suite 240, New York, NY 10011

Cataloging-in-Publication Data

Names: Torres, John, editor.
Title: Critical perspectives on minors playing high-contact sports / edited by
John A. Torres.
Description: New York : Enslow Publishing, 2017. | Series: Analyzing the issues
Includes bibliographical references and index.
Identifiers: ISBN 9780766081376 (library bound)
Subjects: LCSH: Brain — Concussion — Juvenile literature. | Sports injuries —
Juvenile literature.
Classification: LCC RC394.C7 T67 2017 | DDC 617.4'81044 — dc23

Printed in the United States of America

To Our Readers: We have done our best to make sure all website addresses
in this book were active and appropriate when we went to press. However, the
author and the publisher have no control over and assume no liability for the
material available on those websites or on any websites they may link to. Any
comments or suggestions can be sent by e-mail to customerservice@enslow.com

Excerpts and articles have been reproduced with the permission of the copyright
holders.

CONTENTS

INTRODUCTION

Ever since mankind has hunted for sustenance, fought to protect its way of life, and trained in order to survive harsh conditions or long migrations, young people have been involved in what can be considered the equivalent of contact sports training.

Of course, the consequences were life and death back then, not just for sport or to pick a winner.

Today, for the most part, the modern world does not typically require children to don battle helmets, shields, and swords as they prepare for adulthood. No, today those tools have been replaced by football, hockey, or lacrosse helmets, shoulder pads, shin guards, and hockey sticks.

And as science and technology reveal more every year about the dangers that contact sports may present with regard to long-term and immediate head injuries, the debate over allowing children to participate in contact sports continues.

One of the issues in the debate is that the data is so new. This is because for decades, sports-related concussions either went undiagnosed or unreported as the injury was not thought to be anything serious. In years past, players who didn't get right back on the field were considered "soft" or not serious about their team.

Athletes were afraid of losing their positions or being replaced and so often played through injuries, even serious ones. No one, even today, wants to end up like Wally Pipp.

Pipp was the starting first baseman of the New York Yankees baseball team back in the 1920s. He was a very good player but something happened on June 2, 1925, that would change his career forever. Pipp had been hit in the head with a baseball a few weeks earlier and continued to play. When he showed up to the park on June 2, he asked the trainer for some aspirin to treat his headache.

The manager told him to take the day off and treat his headache. He put Lou Gehrig in to take Pipp's place. Gehrig played the next 2,130 consecutive games, basically ending Pipp's career.

Head injuries in sports have long been ignored by coaches and athletes alike. College football coach Bill Curry, who played in the National Football League (NFL) for the Green Bay Packers, said that legendary coach Vince Lombardi had a unique way of treating headaches and head injuries.

According to Curry, he suffered a concussion during a pre-season game after getting kicked in the head. He didn't know where he was or what he was doing and he had to be helped off the field. Less than forty-eight hours later, and with no treatment, Curry showed up at practice and complained of still having a headache.

Lombardi ordered him to put on his gear and meet the fearsome Ray Nitschke out on the playing field. Nitschke was known for being one of the hardest hitters in football and would often use his padded forearm as a weapon, slamming it up against opposing players' helmets. That tactic is no longer allowed in the NFL.

Curry went on to explain that Lombardi ordered Nitschke and him to engage in something called the "Oklahoma drill," which is essentially a one-on-one hitting drill: two players run at each other and hit each other as hard as they can.

They did this repeatedly. After a while, Curry said, his headache was gone.

Many players from the Lombardi era in the 1950s and 1960s have suffered cognitive and brain issues from all the hard hits taken during those days and from the lack of understanding from the trainers and coaches as to the seriousness of these injuries.

None of the players, however, blame Lombardi.

"That was the day of the final cutdown," said Curry. "I guess if I had collapsed, I would not have made the team. Obviously if I had passed away, I would not have made the team. That was the test for concussion. Honestly, that's how it was done. And I don't blame anybody. I don't blame the league, and I don't blame Coach Lombardi. That's just what the culture dictated."

Ironically, Curry has no mental issues, unlike many of his teammates, which raises the question of how important genetics may be to the issue.

The culture has certainly changed and the tide of public opinion has pressured sports leagues from the NFL all the way down to the pee-wee level. But has the pendulum swung too far?

While many are saying the changes regarding contact sports are needed to keep children safe, there are some that say that sports shouldn't be so highly regulated, and kids should be allowed to just be kids on the playing field. This book will help readers view the issue from all sides.

CHAPTER 1

WHAT THE EXPERTS SAY

Most everyone agrees that there is an inherent risk of injury when participating in sports. At the age of forty-eight, I suffered a torn Achilles tendon while playing two-hand-touch football with some of my friends. The non-contact injury caused me to have surgery and miss about nine weeks of work while I recuperated.

I, like most who play sports, knew the risk of injury going in. But, like nearly everyone, I never thought something like that would happen to me.

Each sport has its own set of unique risks. You are not likely to drown playing football but it is a possibility for a swimmer. Football and ice hockey players are likely to have more collision-related injuries than long-distance runners.

Boxers are likely to suffer the highest percentage of head injuries.

It's the nature of the sport. Those are the risks we take when we participate.

But what have academic researchers found?

For the most part, experts in sports medicine are calling for even more research and more studies to be conducted. That is because there still exists some debate as to what constitutes a concussion. Some researchers insist there needs to be a loss of consciousness while others do not.

Regardless, the first study to really examine head injuries in youth sports is believed to be a 1983 study that examined high school football players and their rate of injury. That study may have spurred more in-depth research conducted in the 1980s with the emphasis shifting from just diagnosis to treatment and establishing a protocol for the athlete returning to action.

Today, research continues but conclusions may not be entirely clear. For example, some experts believe that chronic traumatic encephalopathy (CTE), a degenerative brain disease found in the brains of many professional athletes, can only be diagnosed post-mortem. Other experts believe there is a link between CTE and traumatic encephalopathy syndrome (TES), which has been linked with a history of concussions. If CTE and TES are linked, this could provide opportunities to test for degenerative brain disease before an athlete's death.

"CONCUSSION: HORROR OF SPORTS-RELATED BRAIN DAMAGE IS ONLY NOW EMERGING," BY WILLIAM STEWART, FROM *THE CONVERSATION* WITH THE PARTNERSHIP OF THE UNIVERSITY OF GLASGOW, FEBRUARY 5, 2016

Not so long ago, it was a diagnosis that was barely mentioned. Now it feels like there's a plague of concussion in modern sport, with endless news articles and commentaries on the injury and its consequences. There are calls for heading to be banned in children's football and for parents to think again about letting their sons and daughters play rugby. Most recent is an award-winning Hollywood movie on the subject starring Will Smith, imaginatively titled Concussion, which launches in the UK on February 12. So why all the fuss? Should we all be wearing helmets?

Concussions were traditionally seen as causing short-term functional problems like memory loss and impaired concentration. Now people are becoming increasingly aware that they result in structural damage, in particular to fine nerve-cell fibres called axons deep inside the brain.

A further common misperception is that you need to be knocked out to be concussed. In truth, as little as 10% of concussion is associated with loss of consciousness. Concussion is any disturbance in brain function caused by injury, either through direct contact with the head or through whiplash as a result of a blow somewhere else on the body.

The long list of signs and symptoms includes headaches, seizures, memory loss and visual disturbance, of which the commonest is headaches. Symptoms can be delayed, presenting hours or even a day after the event. Yet recent data shows that concussed athletes remaining in play are at increased risk of further injury. This can include non-brain injuries, although they particularly run the risk of worsening their brain injury if they sustain another blow – including the rare complication "second impact syndrome", which can lead to severe complications and even death. "If in doubt, sit it out," is the advice in all sports at all levels.

INCREASED DEMENTIA RISK

Specialists are becoming more aware of the fact that brain injury, including even concussion, increases the risk of degenerative brain disease leading to dementia. Originally thought to be exclusive to retired boxers, this dementia was for many decades recognised as punch-drunk syndrome or dementia pugilistica.

But as the new Will Smith film makes clear, just over a decade ago we began to see cases of the same pathology in other athletes exposed to repetitive concussions, including rugby and soccer. The film tells the story of the first case described in American footballers, and the struggle of pathologist Dr Bennet Omalu (Will Smith) to raise awareness of the condition with the National Football League (NFL).

Following the recognition that it is brain injury rather than a single sport that carries the risk of this degenerative brain disease, the condition is now referred to as chronic traumatic encephalopathy (CTE). But despite increasing reports of CTE in a growing list of sports, as yet there is no diagnostic test. So far, all cases diagnosed have been at post-mortem examination. This has included over 100 former NFL players, for instance.

Undoubtedly there have been many more cases of CTE diagnosed as an alternate dementia. With current best estimates suggesting between 5% and 15% of dementia may be brain-injury related, there are probably many people living now with CTE without knowing it. Do you know a former rugby or soccer player with dementia? With the Six Nations annual rugby tournament getting underway again, it is a sobering thought.

WHAT'S THE CURE?

We are inevitably only at the beginning of understanding CTE. This will gradually change through programmes of research in sports concussion and the pathology of CTE like my one in Glasgow. As this knowledge grows, targets for treatments might emerge, which may also help us treat other similar degenerative brain diseases such as Alzheimer's.

In the absence of a full understanding of the risk factors and with no diagnostic tests or treatments, CTE is one condition that seems best managed by the mantra "prevention is better than cure". The simplest and most effective way of reducing the incidence of this form of dementia might just be to lower the risk of concussion and become better at recognising and managing the injury.

In the meantime, while there may be anxieties about the risks of concussion, there remains no doubt about the lifelong health benefits of sport. As such, my view is that we should continue to encourage wider participation in sport, while promoting better recognition and management of the inevitable concussions. This includes being aware that despite all the technology and research invested in headgear, it still provides no meaningful protection against concussion. But if we approach the problem with the best available knowledge, we can get the benefits of sport while reducing the risks from concussion.

1. At the end of this article, the author states that "prevention is better than cure" for sports-related brain injuries. But he also states that headgear provides no "meaningful protection" against concussions. How can athletes protect themselves while continuing to play high-contact sports?

"ADDRESSING THE LONG-TERM IMPACT OF CONCUSSION IN LIVING PATIENTS," BY HALEY OTTMAN, FROM THE UNIVERSITY OF MICHIGAN HEALTH SYSTEM, JUNE 20, 2016

Much of what's known about CTE stems from postmortem diagnoses. Now, physicians have outlined a framework to identify clinical consequences of head trauma in the living.

One after another, former athletes from high-contact sports have been diagnosed with chronic traumatic encephalopathy, or CTE, upon death. Most played football though a wide spectrum of other sports has been represented as well.

CTE is believed to be a progressive neurodegenerative disease that can only be assessed postmortem. But physicians at Michigan NeuroSport have begun their own clinical approach for living patients who have experienced repeated head trauma. They published a framework in *JAMA Neurology.*

"Health care providers need a way to address patients with a history of repetitive brain trauma who are exhibiting neurologic signs or symptoms," says first author Nicole Reams, M.D., a former sports neurology fellow at the University of Michigan who now practices in Chicago. "Our work aims to provide that clinical construct for living patients."

That diagnosis, called traumatic encephalopathy syndrome, is related to a history of concussions. But a person who has TES may not have CTE, and vice versa. The relationship between the two is unknown.

THE CLINICAL APPROACH

The most important part of determining whether a patient has possible or probable TES is time: two years of symptoms. That helps avoid false positives; this isn't a diagnosis from a single concussion. It's also important to rule out any other neurologic disorder that could be causing the symptoms associated with TES.

The patient has to have a history of head trauma exposure that's repetitive in nature, which typically means a history of concussion.

The physicians look for cognitive dysfunction, behavioral symptoms and mood changes that are progressive, such as:

Depression

Anxiety

Paranoid thoughts

Violence

Socially inappropriate behavior

Declining motor function is related as well, including slowness of motion, or bradykinesia, tremor and instability.

HOW IS TES TREATED?

The various specialties at Michigan NeuroSport come together, from sports neurology to physical medicine and rehabilitation to neuropsychology, to address the patient's individual issues, whether from possible or probable TES.

"We assess comorbid conditions, like obstructive sleep apnea, migraines, mood disorders and substance abuse," says Matthew Lorincz, M.D., Ph.D., associate professor of neurology and co-director of Michigan NeuroSport. "It's important to treat what we can treat to improve the patient's health, since TES itself is believed to be neurodegenerative and progressive."

It could be a CPAP for sleep apnea, vestibular therapists for balance or a neuropsychologist to address behavioral and memory changes.

"A team approach is always best when assessing and managing a complex neurological disease process like TES," says James T. Eckner, M.D., M.S., co-author and U-M assistant professor in physical medicine and rehabilitation.

NEXT STEPS FOR HEAD TRAUMA RESEARCH

Reams notes the understanding of TES is early and evolving.

"With continued research, we'll gain more answers about the prevalence of this syndrome, how much head impact exposure is too much, why some with repetitive impacts develop symptoms and others don't and TES' possible relationship to CTE," she says.

Lorincz adds, "We wrote this framework as a guide to inform clinical practice. The research continues to advance, but if all physicians who see patients with concerns about the long-term consequences of head trauma approach it the same way, it will be easier to see patterns and define the true long-term risks of concussion."

1. What signs or symptoms are associated with traumatic encephalopathy syndrome (TES)?

2. Why might it be important for medical researchers to link TES with chronic traumatic encephalopathy (CTE)?

EXCERPT FROM "TRAUMATIC BRAIN INJURY IN SPORTS: A REVIEW," BY CHRISTOPHER S. SAHLER AND BRIAN D. GREENWALD, FROM *REHABILITATION RESEARCH AND PRACTICE*, 2012

ABSTRACT

Traumatic brain injury (TBI) is a clinical diagnosis of neurological dysfunction following head trauma, typically presenting with acute symptoms of some degree of cognitive impairment. There are an estimated 1.7 to 3.8 million TBIs each year in the United States, approximately 10 percent of which are due to sports and recreational activities. Most brain injuries are self-limited with symptom resolution within one week, however, a growing amount of data is now establishing significant sequelae from even minor impacts such as headaches, prolonged cognitive impairments, or even death. Appropriate diagnosis and treatment according to standardized guidelines are crucial when treating athletes who may be subjected to future head trauma, possibly increasing their likelihood of long-term impairments.

INTRODUCTION

Traumatic brain injury has received increased attention, both in the medical literature and social media, particularly in the field of sports. There are 1.7 million documented TBIs annually, with estimates closer to around 3.8 million [1], 173,285 of which are sports- and recreation-related

TBIs among children and adolescents [2]. As the number of participants in youth sports continues to grow, the incidence of brain injury is proportionally increasing as well [2]. There is a greater awareness of potential short- and long-term sequelae of athletes who suffer brain injuries such as increased propensity for reinjury, cognitive slowing, early onset Alzheimer's, second impact syndrome, and chronic traumatic encephalopathy [3–23]. Federal and State governments, along with many sport's governing bodies are implementing rule and policy changes designed to increase protection of athletes and to standardize medical care. There is an inherent risk in many sports for repetitive head trauma that athletes subject themselves to and it may be up to the physician to protect their well-being. It is important to understand that athletes are a unique demographic of patients who have many behaviors that may differ from the "normal" office patient.

The evaluation and management of an athlete with TBI includes symptoms assessment, medical examination, and neurocognitive testing with serial evaluations over the following days, weeks, to months of recovery. An initial cognitive and physical rest period followed by a gradual increase in physiologic and cognitive stress in asymptomatic athletes is the hallmark of management and change in the paradigm of management. Proper treatment includes accurate assessment and management using current guidelines in an attempt to minimize potential future deleterious effects from TBI. The purpose of this paper is to provide a review of contemporary views of mild traumatic brain injury in sports including definition, epidemiology, pathophysiology, diagnosis, and management including return to play. The timeliness of this paper is apparent now that 37 States have established laws requiring youths who sustain a sporting related brain injury be required to see a physician prior to returning to play; as of August 2011, to the best of the authors' knowledge. Schools, communities, and athletic leagues must be aware of these legislations and follow them appropriately.

DEFINITION

The term mild TBI (mTBI) is now used in place of concussion in the nomenclature according to the Centers for Disease Control and Prevention CDC and the World Health Organization (WHO). Traumatic brain injury is a clinical diagnosis of neurological dysfunction following head trauma. Multiple definitions exist however the CDC defines a mTBI as a complex pathophysiologic process affecting the brain, induced by traumatic biomechanical forces secondary to direct or indirect forces to the head. The American Academy of Neurology (AAN) defines mTBI as a biomechanically induced brain injury resulting in neurologic dysfunction [24]. MTBI results in a constellation of physical, cognitive, emotional, and/or sleep-related symptoms and may or may not involve a loss of consciousness (LOC). Duration of symptoms is highly variable and may last from several minutes to days, weeks, months, or even longer in some cases [25]. There is inherent weakness in all the definitions of mTBI as they are based on clinical evaluation and may be biased by the examiner or examinee.

EPIDEMIOLOGY

According to the CDC, there are 1.7 million documented TBIs each year, with estimates closer to around 3.8 million [1].

Direct medical costs and indirect costs such as lost productivity of TBI totaled an estimated $76.5 billion in the United States in 2000 [26, 27]. Annually, US emergency departments (EDs) treat an estimated 173,285 sports- and recreation-related TBIs among children and adolescents, ages ranging from birth to 19 years averaged over 10 years [2]. During the same 10-year period, ED visits for sports- and recreation-related mTBIs among children and adolescents increased by 60% annually [2], from 153,375 to 248,418 in 2009 [28]. ED visits for mTBI occurring in organized team sports almost doubled in children aged 8 to 13 years and more than tripled among youths aged 14 to 19 years from 1997 to 2007 [29]. Breakdown of these numbers show that 71.0% of all sports- and recreation-related TBI emergency department visits were males and 70.5% of total visits were among persons aged 10–19 years [2]. Overall, the activities most commonly associated with TBI-related ED visits included bicycling and football; followed by playground activities, basketball, and soccer [2,28].

CDC data is not available for non-ED visits which include primary care and specialist office visits because the collection of brain injury data is easier to collect and quantify in ED patients. Increase incidence is multifactorial, and is in part due to the increase in participation of our youth in athletic activities [31]. There is also increased awareness by the general public including parents and coaches to report and refer patients with concussive symptoms for physician evaluation.

CLINICAL PRESENTATION OF TBI IN ATHLETES

The clinical signs and symptoms of mTBIs may range from subtle mood changes to obvious loss of consciousness.

The onset of symptoms may be immediately following the injury, or several minutes later [36]. The AAN identifies signs of mTBI to be amnesia, behavior or personality changes, confabulation, delayed verbal and motor responses, disequilibrium, orientation, emotional labiality, loss of consciousness, slurred/incoherent speech, or a vacant stare. Symptoms of mTBI may include blurry/double vision, confusion, dizziness, excessive drowsiness, sleep difficulties, feeling hazy, foggy, or groggy, headache, inability to focus or concentrate, nausea, vomiting, and photo- or phonophobia [24]. Mood changes, emotional outburst, and behavioral changes also may be the principle manifesting symptoms of mTBI. Mild TBI should also be only a part of a broader differential diagnosis of the previously mentioned signs and symptoms of other common sports-related conditions such as poorly fitting helmet, dehydration, migraine headache, heat exhaustion/stroke, metabolic disturbances, and cardiac or other medical conditions.

Clinicians need consider athletes a unique population subset during evaluations. The sporting world has a culture and mentality that is predicated on pushing athletes beyond their perceived physical and mental abilities. This includes participating in adverse conditions and through a multitude of injuries. Athlete's desire to better themselves and help their team succeed will frequently supersede all other considerations, even at risk to their own bodily harm. Athletes are well known to underreport symptoms that may exclude them from participation. Long standing philosophies such as "getting their bell rung" is often just an accepted part of athletic competition. Other considerations are signs or symptoms of TBI may only be presents under stressful, high exertion game-like conditions. There may also be other incentives and outside motivators to perform well in athletic arena such as the presence of professional scouts, possible scholarships, advancement to a higher-level team, or even money. Coaches may not fully disclose all information attempting to keep key players on the playing field. Parents who desire to see their children perform well may not wish to have their son or daughter pulled from the sporting event. These unique circumstances and conditions must be taken into account by physicians when evaluating athletes.

ON THE FIELD ASSESSMENT AND MANAGEMENT

Sports-related mTBI is a common and challenging injury to diagnose, with a constellation of signs and symptoms that can evolve over hours or days after a concussive episode. Evaluation of mTBI should begin with cervical spine evaluation given the similar mechanism of action in both processes. It is important to note that players who sustain severe head trauma causing a loss of consciousness require prompt, on the field assessment of airway, breathing, circulation, and immediate stabilization of the neck with helmet and shoulder pads left on. Those athletes who have persistent loss of consciousness (LOC) or alteration of consciousness should be kept in a stable position and rapidly transported on a backboard and ambulance to an emergency room. However, most athletes will not suffer LOC and may be evaluated on the sidelines.

Any player suspected of sustaining a mTBI should be immediately removed from the playing field for proper evaluation. If a player has a suspected brain injury and a physician is not present at the venue, the player must be removed from practice or play and referred for proper evaluation before being able to return to play. The point should be made again that most concussions to do involve loss of consciousness. There is also the possibility of delayed symptoms or neurologic decline in these patients, which makes it imperative to perform serial examinations. Multiple studies have shown that collegiate and high school level athletes may demonstrate delayed onset of neuropsychological deficits and symptoms post-injury [37–42]. If the diagnosis of TBI is made, the athlete is required to sit out the remainder of the game or competition. Initial treatment should begin with symptomatic management by reducing the physical and cognitive stressors that may be profound in the sporting arena. The bright lights and loud noises should be minimized which may require removing the athlete completely from the sporting complex. The player initially may require mild analgesics for persistent headache for which Tylenol or NSAIDs may be prescribed. Relative cognitive and complete physical rest should be maintained for at least 24 hours or until follow up evaluation with a physician can be made to begin the return to play protocol.

The paradigm shift in recent years has moved the focus of the initial assessment from grading the severity of the TBI to injury detection and characterization [43]. The scales previously used for grading TBIs have been the Cantu and Colorado guidelines. These guidelines stratify the severity of the TBI based on presence/duration of loss of consciousness (LOC) and presence/duration of amnesia or confusion. Management of that athlete and the RTP is then based on the grade of mTBI they receive at the time of initial assessment, however, this is no longer the current recommended practice.

The primary assessment used today by sports medicine physicians is the SCAT-2 (Sport Concussion Assessment Tool-2), which is a product of the consensus guidelines established in Zurich in 2008 during the 3rd International Conference on Concussion in Sport. Although no prospective studies exist establishing its efficacy, it is believed to be the best screening tool as it incorporates the key components from other scales, and was constructed by the leaders in the field of mTBI in sports in the form of consensus guidelines. Components include review of subjective symptoms, the Glasgow coma scale, the standardized assessment of concussion (SAC) cognitive assessment, Maddocks score, and an evaluation of balance and coordination. Scores of the SCAT-2 can be summated, however clinicians should be mindful that there is not a "normal score" or score cut off to allow RTP (Supplementary material available online at http://dx.doi.org/10.1155/2012/659652). The SCAT-2 is most effective when it is compared to a baseline screen, as well as serial examinations following a TBI. Athletes seen in the office setting undergo detailed evaluation including history and past medical history, neurologic examination focusing on coordination and balance, and cognitive functioning.

In addition to having properly trained medical professionals performing TBI assessments, it is important to ensure coaches, trainers, players, and family are also educated about the possible signs and symptoms to ensure early recognition. Physicians are not present at all the athletic venues in which TBIs may occur such as practices or training sessions. The

CDC has an initiative termed "Heads Up" to educate not only physicians, but also coaches, parents, schools, and athletes on preventing, recognizing, and responding to TBIs. Information includes statistics, fundamentals of TBI, sign and symptom lists, prevention techniques, and treatment protocols with wording that is directed for their respective audience. Also available are pocket size cards with condensed information on recognition, assessment, and management that is available for non-medical professionals to take out in the field. Studies have found that the coaches' version of the toolkit helped them to better identify signs and symptoms of mTBI, increased their awareness of the requirement of health care professional evaluation, and provided helpful information about possible length of recovery [44]. Chrisman et al found physicians were more likely to be aware of and to follow recommended guidelines for RTP activity after reading the Heads Up toolkit than those who did not [45].

NEUROCOGNITIVE EVALUATIONS AND THE ROLE OF BASELINE TESTING

Available baseline cognitive screening tools include neurocognitive testing, Immediate Measurement of Performance and Cognitive Testing (ImPACT), Brain Injury Screening Questionnaire (BISQ), Automated Neuropsychological Assessment Metrics (ANAM), CogSport (formerly Concussion Sentinel), Concussion Resolution Index (CRI), and the Standardized Assessment of Concussion (SAC). Evaluation of many scales including the SCAT-PCSS, IMPACT-PCSS, Signs and Symptoms checklist, Pittsburgh Steelers Post Concussion Scale, Concussion Symptom Inventory, and the Head Injury Scale did not find one particular scale statistically superior to the rest in screening for TBI, however, neurocognitive evaluation was not included [43]. Computerized and traditional neurocognitive testing of verbal and visual memory, complex attention, reaction time, and processing speed is a useful tool to diagnose and to track athletes when baseline testing is performed and compared with post-injury scores [46]. The Zurich consensus guidelines state that neurocognitive testing is the cornerstone to TBI identification and management [47]. Resolution of post-concussive symptoms and return to baseline cognitive status typically are thought to occur on similar timelines [48]. However, when comparison of baseline and post-injury results in a group of collegiate athletes, 83% of athletes with concussions had significantly lower neurocognitive test scores when compared with their baseline scores demonstrating that neurocognitive testing was nearly 20% more sensitive for detecting injury than symptom reporting alone [49]. None of the athletes in the control group had symptoms or lower scores on neurocognitive testing demonstrating a high sensitivity and specificity for neurocognitive testing in identifying concussion. Similar studies have also confirmed these findings demonstrating the "added value" of computerized neurocognitive testing [50]. This clearly identifies the integral role of neurocognitive testing in the management of TBI in the athletic venue. Administration of traditional neuro-psychologic testing to this point has not been available for all athletes mainly due to the financial cost and resources required to administer the examination, specifically a trained neuropsychologist. One solution is through the use of computerized testing which presents many advantages. Computerized neurocognitive testing has been shown to provide sensitive and specific objective data to quantify injury and track recovery [49–51]. Advantages include screening of athletes at a lower financial cost and with only minimal human resource. Also, preseason testing of large numbers of athletes can be now be quickly and efficiently accomplished at most levels of competition. Large databases of information may also be constructed allowing researchers more data for analysis to continue advancing our knowledge in the management of TBI in sports.

Baseline neurocognitive testing is recommended when possible. Cognitive function should be evaluated and tracked following a TBI in an athlete and used as a component in the decision-making management of that player, but never as a sole factor.

RETURN TO PLAY CRITERIA

The key feature of TBI management in sports is physical and cognitive rest until symptoms resolve. A graduating program of exertion and cognitive workload prior to medical clearance and return to play. The basis behind the RTP criteria is that a concussed brain has a lower threshold of reinjury in the first few days or weeks following the initial injury [56]. Recovery times may be longer in adolescents and children [57]. An athlete who returns to play within this vulnerable time period risks permanent disability or even death [58, 59]. Athletes are unique in particular regarding the desire to quickly return to the same venue in which the brain injury was sustained. The RTP guidelines are established to protect the health of the athletes.

Previously, the Cantu and Colorado guidelines were used basing the RTP criteria on severity of mTBI and number of mTBIs that season. Although they take into account the athletes symptoms when returning to play, there were not established guidelines for a graduating stepwise addition of physical and cognitive workload prior to return to play. The current standard of care is based on the consensus guidelines established at the 3rd International Conference on Concussion in Sport in 2008 when determining RTP [...] The guidelines allow for an initial phase of physical and cognitive rest, with slow reintroduction of physical and cognitive activity in a stepwise fashion, providing the patient remains asymptomatic at each step. There are 6 phases in the protocol starting with complete physical and cognitive rest, then advancing to light aerobic exercise, sport-specific exercise, noncontact training drills, full contact practice, and finally RTP. The initial rest period should not only include complete physical rest, but the athlete's academic work also requires modification. This may include, but is not limited to, a reduced number of work assignments, more time to complete class work and tests, breaking down complex tasks into simple steps, and providing a distraction free area for work. A comprehensive medical examination, incorporating SCAT-2, as well as computerized neurocognitive testing should also be conducted at this point. If the athlete is asymptomatic, they may advance to light aerobic exercise (e.g., walking, swimming, stationary cycle) and may continue to progress through the protocol if they remain asymptomatic. If the athlete becomes symptomatic at any point, they must return to the previous level of activity until symptoms resolve for at least 24 hours.

Unrestricted return to play is permitted when the athlete has progressed through the protocol, is asymptomatic, and has returned to baseline or normal values on neurocognitive testing. Given that 90% of mTBI symptoms resolve within one week [41], this protocol can usually be completed in one week as the athlete advances each step in 24 hours. It is recommended to take a more conservative approach to children and adolescents when evaluating for RTP due to particular risks of this age group (i.e., diffuse cerebral swelling) [47]. The guidelines recommend allowing for an extended amount of time of asymptomatic rest and/or the length of graduated exertion in this population. High school athletes had prolonged impairments on neurocognitive testing when compared to professional football players [60] or collegiate athletes [61, 62]. There is evidence that adult brains may be less susceptible to mTBIs and may be able to RTP sooner. Pelman et al. states that some professional American football players are able to RTP more quickly, with even same day RTP supported by National Football League studies without a risk of recurrence or sequelae [63].

It is an important consideration in advancing athletes through the RTP protocol that they remain symptom-free without the use of any pharmacological agents/medications that may mask or modify the symptoms of mTBI [11]. The Zurich consensus guidelines also list modifying factors that require special consideration for RTP criteria and obtaining additional testing such as neuroimaging [...] These include prolonged duration of symptoms, prolonged LOC, seizures, multiple mTBIs especially in the recent past, or change in mental health. Currently, there are no recommendations on the total number of TBIs that are "allowable" for an athlete to sustain before recommending them to sit out the remainder of the season or retiring from the sport. Elite athletes are also recommended to follow the same treatment plan and RTP protocol.

The goal of the guideline is to allow full physical, cognitive, and metabolic recovery to the concussed brain before subjecting it to forces that may cause reinjury. Additional brain trauma within the metabolic recovery window may have both potential short-term and long-term consequences. Even when neuropsychological testing is normal, physiologic, and metabolic dysfunction still may persist for some time. Currently, there are no recommended laboratory testing or imaging modalities that are readily available and reliable to evaluate and follow the microcellular dysfunction. In the future, additional tools may be added into the RTP guidelines such as the previously discussed transcranial Doppler to determine full physiologic recovery.

The evaluation and management of an athlete with TBI is multifactorial assessing symptoms, medical examination, and neurocognitive testing ensuring to catch the variability in presentations of injured athletes. Initial, followed by serial medical and neurocognitive examinations as the patient progresses through the RTP protocol is warranted. Athletes are required to remain fully asymptomatic and returned to baseline cognitive functioning before returning to their sport.

THE SEQUELAE OF TBI IN SPORTS

The increase in media attention, legislation, and constant revision of medical guidelines with respect to TBI is due to the increased awareness of short- and long-term consequences. The obvious immediate impact on the athlete is dealing with the symptoms of a TBI including most commonly headaches, but also poor sleep, excessive drowsiness, poor concentration, and poorer cognitive aptitude. It is estimated that 1.8 million individuals develop acute PTHA each year and 400,000 individuals develop chronic PTHA [64]. Considering most athletes are student-athletes, these symptoms will have an obvious impact on their academic performances as well. In studies of high school and collegiate athletes with a history of three or more concussions had a more severe presentation of concussion, [13] were more likely to have baseline headaches [21], were more vulnerable to brain injury than those without concussion history [4], and were three times more likely to sustain an additional injury [65]. Also, repeated mild TBIs occurring within a short period of time (i.e., hours, days, or weeks) may be catastrophic or fatal [3].

A growing body of evidence exists linking brain injuries of all severity with long-term sequelae.

Repeated mild TBIs occurring over an extended period of time (i.e., months, years) may result in cumulative neurological and cognitive deficits. Retired American professional football players with a history of three or more TBIs were 5 times more likely to have mild cognitive impairment [12]. Professional boxers are well known to have a risk of significant cognitive decline and alterations in brain function [7]. However, there is increasing concern that cumulative effects may also be occurring in athletes who sustain more "routine" injuries as a function of playing a contact sport such as football or ice hockey [8, 9]. Long term effects of repeated concussions include chronic motor and neuropsychological deficits [10, 11]. Collins et al. found that among 400 collegiate football players with two or more previous TBIs independently predicted long-term deficits of executive function, processing speed, and self-reported symptom severity [8]. The nature, burden, and duration of the clinical postconcussive symptoms may be more important than the presence or duration of amnesia alone [14–16]. A telephone-based survey performed by the University of Michigan Institute of Social Research in association of the National Football League of 1,063 retired NFL players found a 19-fold increase rate of memory-related diseases such as Alzheimer's in the 35–49-year-old age group and a 5-year-old increase in ages 50+ when compared to national control groups. Chronic Traumatic Encephalopathy is an entity classically described in former boxers [20, 66], however, there are increasing numbers of case reports described in the literature of athletes in other sports who have a significant history of TBIs [17]. McKee et al. reviewed the autopsy findings of three professional athletes in addition to published reports of 48 cases of suspected CTE and concluded that it is a neuropathologically distinct, slowly progressive tauopathy with a clear environmental etiology [19]. A full discussion is not within the scope of this paper, however, the point should be understood that an association between CTE and TBI is evident within the literature and warrants consideration and future study.

SECOND IMPACT SYNDROME

Second-impact syndrome (SIS) is a rare form of reinjury that occurs prior to the complete resolution of a previous TBI [5]. SIS may result in serious permanent neurologic injury or even death, even if the second impact is only considered to be a minor force. According to the AAN, SIS is a diffuse cerebral dysregulation leading to massive cerebral edema and subsequent herniation. Typically athletes diagnosed with SIS are children or adolescents rather than adults.

Fourteen of the 17 case reports of SIS have occurred in persons less than 20 years old, the others were in a 21 y/o and two 24 years old [6]. This is due to the physiologic differences of children and adolescents compared to adults who have prolonged and diffuse cerebral edema after traumatic brain injury with increased sensitivity to glutamate, increasing their risk to secondary injury [22, 23]. Although rare, SIS has a high associated morbidity and mortality and therefore must be considered.

CLINICAL TRAINING OF CLINICIANS IN SPORTS

As important as having a physician conduct the appropriate brain injury evaluation of an athlete is ensuring the appropriate training of that medical professional conducting the examination. Many studies have concluded that most physicians have little to no knowledge on the accurate diagnosis or management of patients with TBI. Powel et al. found in their study that over 50 percent of patients who presented to the emergency department with TBIs were not accurately identified by ED physicians [67]. Surveys to determine the knowledge of TBI guidelines in primary care physicians found that less than half were up to date with current medical management [45]. Of patients admitted to the hospital for TBI, 9% were allowed to RTP too quickly and 60% were given no advice in regards to RTP [68]. In a survey of the members of the American Society of Sports Medicine, only 30% of physicians treated their patients per the current established guidelines [69]. As the incidence of brain injuries continue to increase, there must also be a concurrent increase and improvement of physician knowledge and training regarding assessment and management of TBI in sports.

PREVENTION OF TBI IN SPORTS

Prevention of TBI is paramount and should be the focus of sporting governing bodies, the athletes, coaching staff, and medical professionals. Two main avenues to accomplish this are through improved protective equipment and rule changes. It has long been understood with literature dating back to the 1960s that hard helmets in sports reduce the incidence of skull fractures and bony head trauma, however, they do not reduce the risk of brain injury [70]. Biomechanical studies which show a reduction in impact forces to the brain with the use of head gear and helmets, but these findings have not been translated to show a reduction in TBI incidence [47]. The use of helmets has been argued to increase brain injury rates through behavioral changes in the athletes who are able to assume a more dangerous playing style and use their helmet as a "weapon" when contacting another player [71]. Clinical evidence that current available protective equipment helps to prevent TBI is not established. Helmets protect against head and facial injury and hence should be recommended for participants in alpine sports [72]. This failure to reduce mTBIs is a product of the biomechanical forces needed to generate the primary neuronal pathology in TBI, diffuse axonal injury (DAI). Helmets are primarily designed to reduce linear accelerative/decelerative forces, not the rotational forces which cause the DAI and in fact may increase rotation forces experienced.

Mouth guards have a definite role in preventing dental and oro-facial injuries [47].

The primary means in which rates of TBI incidence in sports will reduce is through rule changes to minimize head impacts moving forward. Penalizing, fining, or suspending athletes who intentionally impact another players head are means to discourage brain trauma. No longer allowing football (soccer) players to head the ball removes a large risk factor as it has been shown that heading accounts for around 50% of brain injuries in sport [73].

DISCUSSION

Traumatic brain injury continues to be a popular topic in the medical community and social media, especially in youth sports. We have seen double to triple the number of ED visits by children and adolescents for evaluation of sports related TBI in the past ten to fifteen years [74]. It is important to understand that athlete should be considered a unique population with its own culture and risk factors. Maximizing performance is often the primary objective, even if that is at the cost of bodily harm. The prior thinking that mTBI only occurred in contact sports is not correct as demonstrated by the incidence of brain injury in soccer players [2,28, 30, 73]. Cognitive impairments as well as long-term consequences such as early dementia have been linked to recurrent mTBIs and even repetitive subconcussive impacts [8, 9]. Chronic traumatic encephalopathy or second impact syndrome are seen mostly in children and adolescents and are rare but devastating potential sequelae of repetitive brain injuries as well. Protecting athletes using our current understanding of the brain injury model is the primary goal of the medical community serving this group. Under the advisement of the medical community, legislatures have passed laws mandating that youths who are suspected of sustaining a TBI during a game or practice, must be removed from competition and sat out until cleared for RTP by a physician. It is imperative that these athletes are evaluated by a physician trained in sports medicine and familiar with the culture of this subset population. Consensus statement guidelines establish clear management of athletes with TBI and have been outlined in this paper. The evaluation of an athlete with TBI is multifactorial assessing symptoms, medical examination, and neurocognitive testing followed by serial evaluations over the days, weeks, to months of recovery. An initial cognitive and physical rest period, followed by a gradual increase in physiologic and cognitive stress in asymptomatic athletes is the hallmark of management. Athletes are not permitted to return to play until asymptomatic under physiologic stress. Continued education of the general public who may interact with athletes is essential to correctly identify concussed individuals and direct them to appropriate medical care.

Future work should focus on providing evidence to support using the SCAT2 assessment format. Continuing work to improve imaging modalities such as the discussed transcranial Doppler or using serum biomarkers as means to assess and follow physiologic dysfunction and recovery would be excellent additional tools for managing athletes with brain injuries. A better understanding of what and why there appear to be differences in brain injuries in adults compared to children or adolescents and how that would affect RTP management. Presently, the focus should continue to prioritize proper assessment and management by medical professionals based on the current guidelines reviewed in this article, and continued rule changes to minimize head trauma and incidence of brain injury.

1. What are some challenges researchers state that the sports and medical communities face in addressing sports-related brain injuries in young adults and children?

2. What are the two main avenues to prevent continued incidence of traumatic brain injuries (TBI) that the authors of this study suggest?

EXCERPT FROM "SPORTS COACHES NEED TO BE EDUCATED ABOUT CONCUSSION TO KEEP PLAYERS SAFE ON THE FIELD," BY JEFF CARSON AND ANDREW BENNIE, FROM *THE CONVERSATION* WITH THE PARTNERSHIP OF WESTERN SYDNEY UNIVERSITY, AUGUST 1, 2016

WHAT CAN WE DO TO HELP KEEP ATHLETES SAFE FROM CONCUSSION?

Coaches can be key to promoting a supportive environment when it comes to concussion safety and prevention. This is because coaches are among the most influential individuals in an athlete's life.

Their role extends beyond teaching technical and tactical aspects of sport, as they play an integral role in athletes' health, well-being and personal development.

However, researchers have found that coaches lack knowledge about concussions.

For example, an Australian study found that community coaches, who play a fundamental role in young people's initial experiences and safety in sport, were unclear about the common signs and symptoms, management and return-to-activity guidelines associated with sport-related concussions.

HOW ARE COACHES LEARNING ABOUT CONCUSSIONS?

Our research in Canada explored coaches' knowledge about concussions, including how they have acquired information about the injury.

Despite working in an environment with full-time athletic therapists at most practices and all games, the high school coaches in our sample did not feel confident in their knowledge of concussions:

If you asked me all the concussion symptoms right now – I would be guessing. I would be looking at their eyes to see if they're dazed or dilated ... I don't know. I would look for an abnormality in the eyes. But I certainly couldn't list the proper protocol.

The Canadian coaches told us they primarily acquired knowledge through personal experiences (as athletes and now as coaches and parents) and from reading sports media reports of prominent athletes' experiences. One coach said:

I think media reports have changed the way I think about concussions. I take them more seriously. How many times did we get our bell rung and get back into a game? When you hear about the retired football, hockey and rugby players who are describing what they are going through … I'm sure that current players would not want to experience that in their retirement.

None of the coaches in our sample used, or were aware of, the free online educational materials offered through the Coaching Association of Canada (CAC).

The CAC developed a series of online modules aimed at educating coaches about concussions to help them better ensure athletes' safety in training and competition.

However, coaches are not required to complete the modules to gain accreditation. The extent to which these modules have improved athletes' safety from concussions is also not clear.

Similarly, the Australian Sports Commission provides coaches with general information about injuries on its website, but there is little to no information on concussions.

Some independent sporting bodies, such as the Australian Football League and the National Rugby League, have more detailed information about concussion management for their coaches. However, this type of information does not appear to be a mandatory part of their coach education, nor does it appear to be widely available for Australian coaches in other sporting disciplines.

This indicates that important concussion messages are not reaching coaches, which suggests coach certification agencies need to do more to ensure coaches are appropriately educated about the injury, recovery and management processes.

WHAT IS A CONCUSSION AND WHAT INFORMATION ARE COACHES MISSING?

A concussion is a brain injury caused by a direct blow or indirect forces (whiplash, for example) transmitted to the head.

Concussions can involve physical, behavioural and cognitive effects such as dizziness, unsteadiness, irritability, difficulty concentrating and sleep disturbances.

Symptoms typically resolve within two weeks. However, a number of modifying factors (eg history of injury, age) can lead to a prolonged recovery.

Athletes who experience multiple or repeated concussions have been found to experience more severe symptoms, including depression and anxiety. Researchers have begun linking these instances with chronic cognitive impairment.

Researchers have also found that athletes under the age of 18 suffer more severe concussion symptoms than adults. This is concerning given the important cognitive development that occurs throughout adolescence.

Aside from lacking general knowledge of concussions, there are some common misunderstandings among coaches about the injury.

Some coaches believe that athletes must lose consciousness to be concussed, which is not true, and that protective equipment such as helmets/headgear and mouthguards will prevent concussions, which is also not the case.

Coaches are not expected to have the same training as medical doctors, nor should they be considered to be the sole person responsible for dealing with concussion injuries. But they can play a pivotal role in injury recognition and promoting a safe and supportive environment.

WHAT CAN COACHES DO TO HELP ENSURE ATHLETES' SAFETY?

Coaches can ask their local or provincial sport associations for concussion resources, policies and procedures before the season.

They can also take advantage of free educational resources like the concussion recognition tool. Experts developed this to help coaches recognise possible signs and symptoms of a concussion.

This pocket-sized tool can be printed out and carried to the field of play. It is particularly useful for those who do not have access to on-site health professionals (which is the majority of youth sport coaches).

Although only accredited medical and health professionals can make a diagnosis, this tool can empower coaches to help protect their athletes from the potentially catastrophic injuries that can occur when athletes return to play while concussed.

They can also create and foster a sport environment that encourages athletes to accurately report possible concussions.

To help dispel some athletes' fears or apprehensions about accurately reporting concussion symptoms, coaches could develop a protocol that would ensure all athletes have an opportunity to re-establish their position on the team after receiving medical clearance.

1. This expert states that coaches can play a critical role in preventing brain injuries in high-contact sports. Do you agree? Why or why not?

"AS SUICIDES, BRAIN INJURIES MOUNT, SAFETY OF FOOTBALL QUESTIONED, FROM NFL TO YOUTH LEAGUES," FROM *DEMOCRACY NOW!*, FEBRUARY 1, 2013

Ahead of Sunday's Super Bowl, the safety of football is coming under increasing scrutiny as more evidence emerges about links between concussions and brain damage. President Obama recently weighed in on the issue, saying, "If I had a son, I'd have to think long and hard before I let him play football." We speak to former professional wrestler Chris Nowinski, co-founder of the Sports Legacy Institute and co-director of the Center for the Study of Traumatic Encephalopathy at Boston University School of Medicine, which maintains a bank of more than 140 athletes' and military veterans' brains in order to study the effects of concussions. He is the author of the book, "Head Games: Football's Concussion Crisis," which is the focus of a new documentary.

AMY GOODMAN: [You are hearing] Queen, "We Will Rock You," a song often played at football games.

This is *Democracy Now!*, democracynow.org, *The War and Peace Report.* I'm Amy Goodman. As the San Francisco 49ers and Baltimore Ravens prepare for Sunday's Super Bowl, the safety of football is coming under increasing scrutiny as more evidence emerges about links between concussions and brain damage. President Obama recently weighed in on the issue, saying, quote, "If I had a son, I'd have to think long and hard before I let him play football."

Research shows repeated blows to the head can lead to chronic headaches, deteriorating memory, early dementia, and even premature death. Former football All-Pro Rodney Harrison revealed this week he's now, quote, "scared to death," after a career filled with concussions. He spoke with NBC's Bob Costas.

RODNEY HARRIS: I would get up, hit someone. The entire stadium is spinning around. And I will walk to the sideline. They'll hold me out for one play. They'll give me two Advils, and they will tell me, "Get back into the game." The NFL, if they are guilty of anything, it's the lack of awareness that they brought and the lack of education that they told us. They never told us or explained to us or even let us know what a concussion was. I had no idea until just recently.

And even since I retired from the Patriots in 2008, I would still experience headaches. I would play on Sunday, and I would experience headaches up until Tuesday and Wednesday. And even now, at times, there's a sense of loneliness, a sense of isolation, some anxiety problems. And some-times I just—I get headaches. Like even being in bright lights, I get headaches. I'm out golfing. It's tough.

And people have to understand that these players, yeah, a lot of their agendas, it's based on money, but a lot of these players are really, really suffering, Bob. And this stuff is for real, because I'm experiencing it now. I'm scared to death. I have four kids, I have a beautiful wife. And I'm scared to death what may happen to me 10, 15 years from now.

AMY GOODMAN: Former NFL All-Pro Rodney Harrison. While concussions were once an unspoken and misunderstood problem, today more than 4,000 former NFLplayers have filed a lawsuit against the league. They contend the NFL, which makes $9.5 billion a year, knew hits to the head could lead to long-term brain damage but chose not disclose that information.

Meanwhile, new rules are being instituted to mini-mize future injuries. For example, a player can no longer lead with his helmet or hit a defenseless opponent.

For more, we're going to New Orleans, just outside the Super Bowl, to speak with the author of the book on which that film was based. His name is Chris Nowinski, author of *Head Games: Football's Concussion Crisis.* Chris is a former professional wrestler who's become a leading expert on sports-related head injuries, also former football player at Harvard University. He co-founded the Sports Legacy Institute, now co-director of the Center for [the]

Study of Traumatic Encephalopathy at Boston University School of Medicine, which maintains [an] ex-athletes' brain bank to study the effects of concussions.

Chris Nowinski, welcome to *Democracy Now!* You're at the Super Bowl, and you're there to highlight something that is just really beginning to be talked about, as many players bring suit against the National Football League. Can you talk about brain injuries? Can you talk about what it means to have a concussion—what people are probably going to watch a lot of on Sunday?

CHRIS NOWINSKI: Sure. Yeah, I mean, I found out—I had the same experience as Rodney Harrison. I didn't know I was getting concussions my entire career, until it was too late. When I was on the field, whether playing football or wrestling, I'd get hit in the head, and I would black out. I'd forget what I was doing, the sky would go orange, and I would just try to tough it off. And what we've learned through our research at Boston University is that, over time, that can trigger a degenerative brain disease that will eventually, you know, take away your memory, your—your ability to put together sentences, like right today. But in our last study we published in December, 34 of 35 former professional football players had this disease, nine of nine former college players, and even six high school players. So, we're really concerned about the football—the last few generations of football players.

AMY GOODMAN: Now, the league has said for a long time, you know, the players can say, if they get hurt, they don't want to go back in, that it's their responsibility to say they're injured.

CHRIS NOWINSKI: Yeah, that was—and Rodney hit it on the head. It was always a question of education. I did not know the definition of a concussion, even after having a Harvard degree and 19 years of bashing my head, because we've never forced anyone to ever tell an athlete what it means when you get hit in the head and things go fuzzy. And so, the idea—the problem was always informed consent at the beginning. And that's why Ted Johnson, who was one of the first players to come forward, the former New England Patriot, stepped forward. He said, you know, "At least let me make this decision for myself." And so, in 2010, the NFL finally did start educating the players. And so, now it's a different ball game at the pro level, but what really needs to have a light shined on is the fact that there is no such thing as informed consent for children. And 95 percent of the people playing football in this country are under the age of consent, they're under 18. And that's where we really should be focusing.

AMY GOODMAN: Well, let's talk—let's talk about that for a minute. I bet there are a lot of moms and dads and kids who are listening right now. What about a family whose kid is just really good in football and in high school? Maybe they're even being head-hunted right now for the big leagues. What do you say?

CHRIS NOWINSKI: I say it's a huge risk right now. It's—your child surviving youth football is right now mostly luck, because there are so few standards in place to actually protect them. Consider the fact that yesterday the NFL and NFLPA announced they will now have independent neurologists on the sideline because they do not trust the team doctors to make a judgment about whether or not someone who has a concussion can go back in. That's the level of safety we have in the NFL. They even pay an athletic trainer to sit in the sky-box to watch the television feed, because they miss so many concussions on the field. If that's what these millionaires need to protect themselves—your child has no medical pro-fessionals, coaches with no training. You know, their young developing brain is more sensitive to the trauma. And so, from that perspective, you wonder how you could expose children to a game that we think is killing adults.

AMY GOODMAN: Chris Nowinski, can you talk about this unprecedented lawsuit that has been filed against the NFL?

CHRIS NOWINSKI: Yeah, I mean, personally, with our role, we kind of stay out of this. But from what's been happening, is former players who did suffer these injuries on the job are suing the league for not warning them and then not taking care of them. You know, the reality is, you know, when I wrote the first edition of *Head Games* in 2006, I was appalled by the fact that, you know, chronic traumatic encephalopathy—this disease was originally called "punch drunk" in 1928. But we never looked into football, and everyone just assumed football would avoid it.

We knew that putting players back into the game was very bad for their brains when they had concus-sions, but we did it. You know, the 1937 American Foot-ball Coaches Association minutes talk about the fact that they're saying, "We've got to stop putting guys back in. We've got to stop putting guys back in." And it was 72 years later when that became the policy. So, you know, I don't know what exactly happened, but, you know, there's a lot of guys suffering that need care, and I understand why they're suing.

AMY GOODMAN: I want to turn to an excerpt from the documentary *Head Games*, based on your book, Chris, by the same name.

ALAN SCHWARZ: It's been known for a long time that banging your head over and over and over and over again can be a bad thing.

CHRIS NOWINSKI: And I remember I hit the ground, and I forgot where we were. I forgot what we were doing in the ring. I forgot what was coming next. I had been gladly exposing myself to repetitive brain trauma concussions for 19 years.

Members of the committee, this Friday night over a million kids will take to the football field. I am certain that radical measures are needed for football to continue safely.

REP. MAXINE WATERS: No matter what kind of helmet you build, it is a dangerous sport.

UNIDENTIFIED: Co-captain of the Penn football team committed suicide. He had 20 areas of his brain that were falling apart, that were all going to keep spreading.

ANNOUNCER: Whoa! Primeau got levelled!

KEITH PRIMEAU: I know that I damaged my brain. I don't know where I am 10 years from now. I don't know where I am 20 years from now.

CINDY PARLOW-CONE: After I had my first concussion, every time I would do heading, I would see stars.

GIRL SOCCER PLAYER: I was just like, "Oh, my god, my head hurts so bad."

MOTHER 1: She didn't pull herself out of the game. She didn't tell the coach. And she didn't tell us.

BOY HOCKEY PLAYER: I got hit from behind. People said I was on the ice for like four or five minutes. I only remember 20 seconds of it.

UNIDENTIFIED: That's your brain. How much of you are you willing to put on the line for a game?

BOB COSTAS: But what's the level of acceptableness? And what is the level of reasonable reform?

CHRIS NOWINSKI: If you only have one out of every hundred kids getting diagnosed with a concussion, you're missing them, and your kids are at terrible risk.

MOTHER 2: I might look back and say I wished I had stopped him after this last concussion. He loved to play hockey, and we loved watching him play hockey.

MOTHER 3: I believe you just have to protect them as much as you can and—and pray.

AMY GOODMAN: An excerpt of *Head Games,* based on our guest Chris Nowinski's book by the same title. Chris, journalist Paul Barrett has a new article out in *Businessweek* called

"Will Brain Injury Lawsuits Doom or Save the NFL?" In it, he writes, quote, "New research suggests the peril players face may not be limited to car wreck hits. It may extend to the relentless, day-in-and-day-out collisions that are the essence of the game. If science one day determines [that] merely playing serious tackle football substantially increases the danger of debilitating brain disease—as smoking cigarettes makes lung cancer much more likely—it's conceivable [that] the NFL could go the way of professional boxing." Chris Nowinski, what's your response?

CHRIS NOWINSKI: I think that's an accurate portrayal of the situation. You know, football has a very short window to reform itself, especially at the youth level, so that we can feel comfortable exposing kids to this game. You know, pretty soon we're going to be able to diagnose CTE in living people. And the day we do that, and the day we scan a high school football team, and if we find 10, 20, 30 percent of kids with this degenerative brain disease before the age of 18, I think, you know, the games will have a very, very short future after that. So, you know, football needs to reform, and reform quickly.

Today we're going to be actually doing a press conference talking about the fact that the only place that—one of the only places that doesn't set any limits to how frequently and how many days you can hit each other is high school football. For example, in the state of Illinois where I played high school football, we weren't allowed to hit in the summer. Now, Illinois has 20 days of summer contact. It's kind of bizarre.

AMY GOODMAN: Chris, a lot of people have learned about this through the suicides of football players. And one of those football players who actually shot himself, but instead of shooting himself in the head, shot himself in the chest, because he wanted his—he wanted to donate his brain to science to study.

CHRIS NOWINSKI: Yeah, Dave Duerson, a former Chicago Bear. I actually grew up in Chicago, so I grew up watching him. And he actually gave me a scholarship when I was 17, from the National Football Foundation. He, you know, was one of the most successful guys post-NFL career, was on the board of trustees at Notre Dame, ran a multimillion-dollar food distribution. At 45, started having problems with headaches, memory issues, and especially impulse control—got violent with his family, got violent with his children. His wife divorced him. He ended up $20 million in debt. And, you know, left a note asking for us to study his brain, so, I think—so that we could show it wasn't him, the Dave Duerson we all knew, that did all those terrible things. And it wasn't. He had an advanced case of CTE. It was very tragic.

AMY GOODMAN: Again, CTE, chronic traumatic encephalopathy. Chris Nowinski, your Sports Legacy Institute and your work at Boston University now, you are—you have the brains of various football players? You are collecting this as evidence?

CHRIS NOWINSKI: Right, because, you know, there never was a center in the world dedicated to this disease. And the beginning of the study of any disease has to start with knowing what you're dealing with. And so we started this brain bank in 2008. We now have the brains of over 140 athletes, over 100 of which have turned up positive for this disease—not just football players: ice hockey players, rugby players, boxing, professional wrestling, and some more sports that we're going to introduce this year. And it's not just even just athletes: military veterans, battered spouses, epileptics with dozens of falls. So it's—you know, this is a disease that we didn't pay attention to, we didn't understand, and now we really have to catch up and confront.

AMY GOODMAN: Chris Nowinski, I want to thank you so much for being with us and for your work. He's a former Harvard football player, former professional wrestler, leading expert on sports-related head injuries, author of *Head Games: Football's Concussion Crisis*, now co-founded the Sports Legacy Institute.

1. When asked about the risk of youths playing football, Chris Nowinski states, "[Y]our child surviving youth football is right now mostly luck." What do you think with his assessment? Do you think the situation is as serious as Nowinski states?

2. Would Nowinski's statements about the brain injury risk for youths playing contact sports, in particular, deter you from playing? Why or why not?

CHAPTER 2

WHAT THE GOVERNMENT SAYS

There is perhaps no one more powerful in the US government than the president. And even the person occupying the most important office in the land has chimed in when it comes to the dangers of contact sports.

In 2014, US president Barack Obama called for more research into youth concussion and especially for more research to determine the long-term effects of head injuries to young people.

"We want our kids participating in sports," Obama said. "As parents, though, we want to keep them safe and that means we have to have better information."

The president's remarks and attention to the issue clearly elevated the national conversation. But he also admitted that there is a "public

health interest" in having young children participate in sports, which can increase other aspects of
one's health, including lowering the risk of obesity
and decreasing blood pressure, stress, and rates
of depression.

Some states, like Illinois and Arizona, have
taken a leading role in passing comprehensive laws
to protect students from sports-related brain injuries.

The CDC or Centers for Disease Control—a
government agency concerned with the health and
well-being of American citizens—has taken the
lead in getting the right information out to parents,
coaches, and athletes. Their "Heads Up" campaign
aims at minimizing the risk of concussions or other
brain injuries while participating in sports.

EXCERPT FROM "REMARKS BY THE PRESIDENT AT THE HEALTHY KID AND SAFE SPORTS CONCUSSION SUMMIT," BY PRESIDENT BARACK OBAMA, FROM THE WHITE HOUSE OFFICE OF THE PRESS SECRETARY, MAY 29, 2014

THE PRESIDENT: I want to welcome everybody here to
the White House. I want to thank members of Congress,
who are here. We've got leaders from America's sports
and medical communities, especially young people here
like Tori, who did such a great job sharing her story today.

All across the country, there are millions of young athletes just like Tori who spend their weekends and summers on baseball diamonds and soccer pitches. And they put in extra practice so they can make the varsity or maybe even earn a college scholarship. Most of them are not as good as Tori was at her sport. I certainly wasn't -- although, I had the same enthusiasm. And for so many of our kids, sports aren't just something they do; they're part of their identity. They may be budding scientists or entrepreneurs or writers, but they're also strikers and linebackers and point guards. And that's a good thing.

First of all, the First Lady thinks everybody needs to move. (Laughter.) And obviously there's a huge public health interest in making sure that people are participating in sports. But sports is also just fundamental to who we are as Americans and our culture. We're competitive. We're driven. And sports teach us about teamwork and hard work and what it takes to succeed not just on the field but in life.

And I was a basketball player -- as I said, not as good as Tori was at soccer. But I learned so many lessons playing sports that I carry on to this day, even to the presidency. And still, when I need to relax and clear my head, I turn to sports -- whether it's a pick-up basketball game -- and I'm much slower than I was just last week -- (laughter) -- or more sedate pastimes like golf, or watching SportsCenter.

And more than that, as a parent, Michelle and I have always encouraged our girls to play sports. One of the greatest transformations I think in our society has been how young women have been finally given the opportunity because of Title IX, and now you see just unbelievable women athletes who are getting the same exposure and experience and outlets for sports all across the country. And Malia and Sasha are part of that generation. They took for granted -- of course, we're playing sports. And they played everything from soccer to basketball and tennis and track. So sports are important to our life as a family, just like they are for families all across the country.

The reason we're here today, though, is all across the country parents are also having a more troubling conversation, and that's about the risks of concussions. There's a lot of concern, but there's a lot of uncertainty. And as Tori's story suggests, concussions are not just a football issue. They don't just affect grown men who choose to accept some risk to play a game that they love and that they excel at. Every season, you've got boys and girls who are getting concussions in lacrosse and soccer and wrestling and ice hockey, as well as football. And, in fact, the Center for Disease Control reports that in the most recent data that's available to us, young people made nearly 250,000 emergency room visits with brain injuries from sports and recreation -- 250,000. That number obviously doesn't include kids who see their family doctor or, as is typical, don't seek any medical help.

Before the awareness was out there, when I was young and played football briefly, there were a couple of times where I'm sure that that ringing sensation in my head and the need to sit down for a while might have been a mild concussion, and at the time you didn't think anything of it. The awareness is improved today, but not by much. So the total number of young people who are impacted by this early on is probably bigger than we know.

Now, I say this not to scare people. We want our kids participating in sports. I'd be much more troubled if young people were shying away from sports. As parents, though, we want to keep them safe, and that means we have to have better information. We have to know what these issues are. And the fact is, we don't have solid numbers, and that tells me that at every level we're all still trying to fully grasp what's going on with this issue.

Last fall, a comprehensive report found that there are too many gaps in the understanding of the effects and treatment for concussions. Researchers are still learning about the causes and consequences of these injuries. Communities are wondering how young it is to start tackle football, for example. Parents are wondering whether their kids are learning the right techniques, or wearing the best safety equipment, or whether they should sign up for -- to have their kids participate in any full-contact sports at all.

We've got some outstanding scientists here today like Francis Collins, the head of the NIH. There may be tests that at some point we can do to see if there is a particular susceptibility to concussions. Some people's brains may be more vulnerable to trauma than others are. We don't know that yet, but there may be some evidence that is worth exploring.

So with all of these questions swirling around, as a parent and as a fan, and in discussions with a lot of other parents and fans who happen to be in this White House, we decided why not use our convening power to help find some more answers. And today we've brought together the President of the NCAA, the MLS commissioner, senior leadership from the NHL, and US Soccer, and the NFL, and the NFL Players Association. We've also got some of the nation's foremost brain experts. We've got doctors who work with kids every day from all over the country. We've got leaders in Pop Warner, and Little League, and Under Armour, and ESPN participating. And we've got members of Congress like Joyce Beatty, and Tim Bishop, and Bill Pascrell, all who have taken a great interest in this.

And because we're all here and are looking for information, even if we may not agree on everything, the one thing we can agree on is, is that sports are vital to this country and it's a responsibility for us to make sure that young, talented kids like Tori are able to participate as safely as possible and that we are doing our job, both as parents and school administrators, coaches, to look after them the way they need to be looked after. That's job number one.

The good news is, across the country people eagerly signed up to participate here. They recognize this is an issue that is worth paying attention to. We've seen all 50 states pass laws requiring concussed athletes to get a medical clearance before they return to play. Folks from USA Hockey banned checking before 12 years old. In March, the NFL donated $45 million to USA Football for their Heads Up Football program, which emphasizes coach training and player safety.

On our part, this administration -- the CDC has spearheaded a public awareness campaign for parents, and athletes, and coaches, and school staff called "Heads Up." And you can check it out at CDC.gov/concussion. That's where we've compiled a lot of the best information available for parents. And while the number of concussions reported among young athletes has risen over the past decade, one reason is likely because players, coaches, and parents better understand symptoms of these injuries.

Still, there's more work to do. We've got to have better research, better data, better safety equipment, better protocols. We've got to have every parent and coach and teacher recognize the signs of concussions. And we need more athletes to understand how important it is to do what we can to prevent injuries and to admit them when they do happen. We have to change a culture that says you suck it up. Identifying a concussion and being able to self-diagnose that this is something that I need to take care of doesn't make you weak -- it means you're strong.

At the same time, I want to point out that this is not just a matter for athletes. You'll notice this big guy here, Ray Odierno, who is not only the leader of our Army, but also is somebody who plays football -- I don't know if he still plays, although he could. (Laughter.) But as a leader of our Armed Forces, he sees the effects that injuries have had on brave men and women who serve in uniform, and all of us who care about them. That's why Ray is here today.

And I've seen in my visits to wounded warriors, traumatic brain injury is one of the signature issues of the wars in Iraq and Afghanistan. The thing is, the vast majority of mild traumatic brain injury cases in the military occur outside deployment. So even though our wars are ending, addressing this issue will continue to be important to our Armed Forces. And as part of a new national action plan we announced last year, we're directing more than $100 million in new research to find more effective ways to help prevent, diagnose and treat mental health conditions and traumatic brain injury -- because the more we can learn about the effects of brain injuries, the more we can do to help our courageous troops and veterans recover. And that obviously gives us more information about our kids, as well.

Today, by the way, I'm proud to announce a number of new commitments and partnerships from the folks in this room that are going to help us move the ball forward on this issue. The NCAA and the Department of Defense are teaming up to commit $30 million for concussion education and a study involving up to 37,000 college athletes, which will be the most comprehensive concussion study ever. And our service academies -- Army, Navy, Air Force, and Coast Guard -- are all signed up to support this study in any way that they can.

The NFL is committing $25 million of new funding over the next three years to test strategies like creating health and safety forums for parents, and they're building on the program piloted by my own Chicago Bears to get more trainers at high school games. And the NIH is announcing the next step in this partnership with the NFL. They're dedicating $16 million of the NFL's previous donation toward studies and clinical trials to examine the chronic effects of repetitive concussions.

The National Institute of Standards and Technology will invest $5 million over the next five years to explore the development of lighter and smarter and more responsive materials for protective equipment. And I want to single out the New York Giants chairman, Steve Tisch, who is here and is donating $10 million of his own money to expand the Brain-

SPORT Program at UCLA to prevent, study, and treat concussions and traumatic brain injury in youth. So all these new commitments are terrific, and we want to thank everybody here for participating. (Applause.)

So just to wrap up, so you can hear from people who actually know what they're talking about, these efforts are going to make a lot of difference for a lot of people -- from soldiers on the battlefield to students out on the football field. Take the Levine family from Rockville, Maryland, who are here today. Where did they go? There they are right there. Cheryl and Jason Levine have three boys, who when you look at them you know right away they're brothers -- Isaac, Sidney, and Rueben. They have loved ice hockey since they were really young.

But when he was seven years old, Sidney suffered a pair of moderate concussions on the ice. A few years later, when Isaac was an eighth grader, he suffered a more severe concussion in a game. After the injury, both boys had headaches. They started struggling in class. They started acting out. Isaac's concussion even kept him out of school for a while. And, as you might imagine, Cheryl was horrified; as she put it, "you only have one brain." That's a good point. And you want to make sure that you're treating it right.

Fortunately, with the help of their doctors, both boys' health and behavior improved. And Sidney was back on the ice 10 weeks after his concussion. He's hoping to play varsity next year as a freshman. And last winter, Isaac played forward as his high school team won the state championship.

Now, Cheryl and Jason could have pulled their boys out -- it was such a scare -- and had their doctors recommended it, that's what they would have done. But they knew that just like millions of kids across the country, kids love their sports. So Cheryl and Jason educated themselves on the issue, and with their doctor's blessing and the support of the coaches and teachers, they're encouraging their boys to lace up those skates and get out on the ice. And as Cheryl said, "My kids aren't going to go on and play in the NHL." I hope they know that, by the way. (Laughter.) "But what I'm worried about is getting through their teens while having fun and building confidence and doing the things they want to do, obviously within certain limits." That's some good parenting by Cheryl.

That's what today is about -- is to give parents the information they need to help their kids compete safely. Let's keep encouraging our kids to get out there and play sports that they love, and doing it the right way. That's not a job just for parents, but it's a job for all of us. And that's why the public-private partnerships like these are important. In a few minutes, I know that many of you are going to take this discussion a step further with this panel of experts moderated by Pam Oliver, which we're very grateful for.

But I want to thank all of you for coming here today, for your contributions to our kids' future. And, most of all, I want to thank the young people who are here, particularly Tori, for highlighting why this issue is so important. We're really excited. And, by the way, Tori although is not going to be playing soccer when she goes to college -- she's graduating -- she does intend to stay involved in the sport, and I understand is going to be doing some coaching of some four- and five-year-olds this summer. And she is going to pass on some of the knowledge, hard-earned knowledge that she's learned. And that's why we know she's going to be a terrific success in whatever she chooses to do.

Thank you, everybody. (Applause.)

1. President Obama, unlike Chris Nowinski, states that he would not suggest that parents pull their kids from high-contact sports teams. Why? Do you agree or disagree?

"PARENT AND ATHLETE CONCUSSION INFORMATION SHEET," FROM THE CENTERS FOR DISEASE CONTROL'S HEADS UP PROGRAM

WHAT IS A CONCUSSION?

A concussion is a type of traumatic brain injury that changes the way the brain normally works. A concussion is caused by a bump, blow, or jolt to the head or body that causes the head and brain to move quickly back and forth. Even a "ding," "getting your bell rung," or what seems to be a mild bump or blow to the head can be serious.

65

WHAT ARE THE SIGNS AND SYMPTOMS OF CONCUSSION?

Signs and symptoms of concussion can show up right after the injury or may not appear or be noticed until days or weeks after the injury.

If an athlete reports one or more symptoms of concussion after a bump, blow, or jolt to the head or body, s/he should be kept out of play the day of the injury. The athlete should only return to play with permission from a health care professional experienced in evaluating for concussion.

DID YOU KNOW?

• Most concussions occur without loss of consciousness.

• Athletes who have, at any point in their lives, had a concussion have an increased risk for another concussion.

• Young children and teens are more likely to get a concussion and take longer to recover than adults.

SYMPTOMS REPORTED BY ATHLETE:

- Headache or "pressure" in head
- Nausea or vomiting
- Balance problems or dizziness
- Double or blurry vision
- Sensitivity to light
- Sensitivity to noise
- Feeling sluggish, hazy, foggy, or groggy
- Concentration or memory problems
- Confusion
- Just not "feeling right" or is "feeling down"

SIGNS OBSERVED BY COACHING STAFF:

- Appears dazed or stunned
- Is confused about assignment or position
- Forgets an instruction
- Is unsure of game, score, or opponent
- Moves clumsily
- Answers questions slowly
- Loses consciousness (even briefly)
- Shows mood, behavior, or personality changes
- Can't recall events prior to hit or fall
- Can't recall events after hit or fall

CONCUSSION DANGER SIGNS

In rare cases, a dangerous blood clot may form on the brain in a person with a concussion and crowd the brain against the skull. An athlete should receive immediate medical attention if after a bump, blow, or jolt to the head or body s/he exhibits any of the following danger signs:

• One pupil larger than the other
• Is drowsy or cannot be awakened
• A headache that gets worse
• Weakness, numbness, or decreased coordination
• Repeated vomiting or nausea
• Slurred speech
• Convulsions or seizures
• Cannot recognize people or places
• Becomes increasingly confused, restless, or agitated
• Has unusual behavior
• Loses consciousness (even a brief loss of consciousness should be taken seriously)

WHAT SHOULD YOU DO IF YOU THINK YOUR ATHLETE HAS A CONCUSSION?

1. If you suspect that an athlete has a concussion, remove the athlete from play and seek medical attention. Do not try to judge the severity of the injury yourself. Keep the athlete out of play the day of the injury and until a health care professional, experienced in evaluating for concussion, says s/he is symptom-free and it's OK to return to play.

2. Rest is key to helping an athlete recover from a concussion. Exercising or activities that involve a lot of concentration, such as studying, working on the computer, and playing video games, may cause concussion symptoms to reappear or get worse. After a concussion, returning to sports and school is a gradual pro-

cess that should be carefully managed and monitored by a health care professional.

3. Remember: Concussions affect people differently. While most athletes with a concussion recover quickly and fully, some will have symptoms that last for days, or even weeks. A more serious concussion can last for months or longer.

WHY SHOULD AN ATHLETE REPORT SYMPTOMS?

If an athlete has a concussion, his/her brain needs time to heal. While an athlete's brain is still healing, s/he is much more likely to have another concussion. Repeat concussions can increase the time it takes to recover. In rare cases, repeat concussions in young athletes can result in brain swelling or permanent damage to their brain. They can even be fatal.

1. The federal government seems to be taking the approach that the best preventative to brain injuries in youth high-contact sports is knowledge of the risks and symptoms associated with concussions. Do you think this is the best way to tackle the issue? Why or why not?

EXCERPT FROM "THE CONCUSSION TREATMENT AND CARE TOOLS ACT OF 2015," INTRODUCED TO THE US SENATE DURING THE 114ᵀᴴ CONGRESS BY SENATOR ROBERT MENENDEZ, FEBRUARY 4, 2016

To amend title III of the Public Health Service Act to provide for the establishment and implementation of guidelines on best practices for diagnosis, treatment, and management of mild traumatic brain injuries (MTBIs) in school-aged children, and for other purposes.

IN THE SENATE OF THE UNITED STATES

January 29, 2015

Mr. MENENDEZ introduced the following bill; which was read twice and referred to the Committee on Health, Education, Labor, and Pensions

A BILL

To amend title III of the Public Health Service Act to provide for the establishment and implementation of guidelines on best practices for diagnosis, treatment, and management of mild traumatic brain injuries (MTBIs) in school-aged children, and for other purposes.

Be it enacted by the Senate and House of Representatives of the United States of America in Congress assembled,

SECTION 1. SHORT TITLE.

This Act may be cited as the "Concussion Treatment and Care Tools Act of 2015" or the "ConTACT Act of 2015".

SEC. 2. FINDINGS.

Congress finds the following:

(1) Concussions are mild traumatic brain injuries, the long-term effects of which are not well understood.

(2) According to the Centers for Disease Control and Prevention (CDC), each year United States emergency departments treat an estimated 173,285 sports- and recreation-related mild traumatic brain injuries (MTBIs), including concussions, among children and adolescents, from birth to 19 years of age. However, this number does not capture the total number, as many MTBIs go undiagnosed.

(3) There is an increased risk for subsequent brain injuries among persons who have had at least one previous brain injury.

(4) A repeat concussion, one that occurs before the brain recovers from a previous concussion, can slow recovery or increase the likelihood of having long-term problems.

(5) In rare cases, repeat concussions can result in second impact syndrome, which can be marked by brain swelling, permanent brain damage, and death.

(6) Recurrent brain injuries and second impact syndrome are highly preventable.

(7) Many States have adopted concussion management rules and regulations, but many schools lack the

resources to implement best practices in concussion diagnosis and management.

SEC. 3. GUIDELINES ON BEST PRACTICES FOR DIAGNOSIS, TREATMENT, AND MANAGEMENT OF MILD TRAUMATIC BRAIN INJURIES IN SCHOOL-AGED CHILDREN.

Part B of title III of the Public Health Service Act 6 (42 U.S.C. 243 et seq.) is amended by inserting after section 317T the following:

"SEC. 317U. GUIDELINES ON BEST PRACTICES FOR DIAGNOSIS, TREATMENT, AND MANAGEMENT OF MILD TRAUMATIC BRAIN INJURIES IN SCHOOL-AGED CHILDREN.

"(a) GUIDELINES.—

"(1) BY SECRETARY.—Not later than 90 days after issuance of the final report under paragraph (2), the Secretary shall establish guidelines for States on the implementation of best practices for diagnosis, treatment, and management of MTBIs in school-aged children.

"(2) BY PANEL.—Not later than July 31, 2015, the Pediatric MTBI Guideline Expert Panel of the Centers for Disease Control and Prevention shall issue a final report on best practices for diagnosis, treatment, and manage-ment of MTBIs in school-aged children.

"(3) STUDENT ATHLETES RETURNING TO PLAY.— The guidelines under paragraph (1) and the report under paragraph (2) shall address best practices for diagnosis, treatment, and management of MTBIs in student athletes returning to play after an MTBI.

"(b) Grants To States.—

"(1) IN GENERAL.—After establishing the guidelines under subsection (a)(1), the Secretary may make grants to States for purposes of—

"(A) adopting such guidelines, and disseminating such guidelines to elementary and secondary schools; and

"(B) ensuring that elementary and secondary schools—

"(i) implement such guidelines;

"(ii) are adequately staffed with athletic trainers and other medical professionals necessary to implement such guidelines; and

"(iii) implement computerized pre-season baseline and post-injury neuropsychological testing for student athletes.

"(2) GRANT APPLICATIONS.—

"(A) IN GENERAL.—To be eligible to receive a grant under this section, a State shall submit an application to the Secretary at such time, in such manner, and containing such information as the Secretary may require.

"(B) MINIMUM CONTENTS.—The Secretary shall require that an application of a State under subparagraph (A) contain at a minimum—

"(i) a description of the strategies the State will use to disseminate the guidelines under subsection (a)(1) to elementary and secondary schools, and to ensure implementation of such guidelines by such schools, including any strategic partnerships that the State will form; and

"(ii) an agreement by the State to periodically provide data with respect to the incidence of MTBIs and second impact syndrome among student athletes in the State.

"(3) UTILIZATION OF HIGH SCHOOL SPORTS ASSO-
CIATIONS AND LOCAL CHAPTERS OF NATIONAL BRAIN
INJURY ORGANIZATIONS.—The Secretary shall require
States receiving grants under this section to utilize, to
the extent practicable, applicable expertise and services
offered by high school sports associations and local chapters of national brain injury organizations in such States.

"(c) Coordination Of Activities.—In carrying out this
section, the Secretary shall coordinate in an appropriate
manner with the heads of other Federal departments and
agencies that carry out activities related to MTBIs.

"(d) Report To Congress.—Not later than 4 years after
the date of the enactment of this section, the Secretary
shall submit to Congress a report on the implementation
of subsection (b) and shall include in such report—

"(1) the number of States that have adopted the
guidelines under subsection (a)(1);

"(2) the number of elementary and secondary
schools that have implemented computerized pre-season
baseline and post-injury neuro-psychological testing for
student athletes; and

"(3) the data collected with respect to the incidence of MTBIs and second impact syndrome among
student athletes.

"(e) Definitions.—In this section, the following
definitions apply:

"(1) The term 'MTBI' means a mild traumatic
brain injury.

"(2) The term 'school-aged child' means an individual in the range of 5 through 18 years of age.

"(3) The term 'second impact syndrome' means
catastrophic or fatal events that occur when an individual

suffers an MTBI while symptomatic and healing from a previous MTBI.

"(4) The term 'Secretary' means the Secretary of Health and Human Services, acting through the Director of the Centers for Disease Control and Prevention.

"(5) The term 'State' means each of the 50 States and the District of Columbia.

"(6) The term 'student athlete' means a school-aged child in any of the grades 6th through 12th who participates in a sport through such child's elementary or secondary school.

"(f) AUTHORIZATION OF APPROPRIATIONS.—To carry out this section, there are authorized to be appropriated $5,000,000 for fiscal year 2016 and such sums as may be necessary for each of fiscal years 2017 through 2020.".

1. This proposed bill was blocked in the Senate and has not been enacted. Why do you think this bill would have been blocked?

"COMMITTEE HEARS TESTIMONY ON PASCRELL'S YOUTH SPORTS CONCUSSION ACT," FROM BILL PARCEL, THE HOUSE OF REPRESENTATIVES, MAY 24, 2016

WASHINGTON – Today, U.S. Rep. Bill Pascrell, Jr. (NJ-09) reacted to consideration of the Youth Sports Concussion

Act, bipartisan legislation aimed at protecting young athletes from the dangers of sports-related traumatic brain injuries. The bill, H.R. 4460, was heard today by the House Committee on Energy and Commerce's Subcommittee on Commerce, Manufacturing, and Trade. The Senate version of the legislation authored by Senator Udall (D-NM) was passed out of the Senate Commerce Committee in April and is awaiting action on the Senate floor.

"Despite some sports leagues keeping their heads in the sand, we are learning more and more every day about traumatic brain injury and other side effects, regardless of the fact that contact sports have dangerous side effects on participants and when the participants are children with still-developing minds and bodies, the dangers can be exaggerated," *said Pascrell*, co-founder and co-chair of the Congressional Brain Injury Task Force. "The federal government must crack down on false advertising and ensure our kids' sports equipment is not being misrepresented as safe. The minds of the next generation are on the line, so the stakes are high and we need action."

Among the testimony heard today by the Energy and Commerce subcommittee (video and documents here), was *Federal Trade Commission Chairwoman Edith Ramirez*.

"H.R. 4460, the Youth Sports Concussions Act, would give the FTC civil penalty authority, and authorize actions by states, to address the importation and sale of sports equipment for which the importer or seller has made deceptive safety benefit claims. The Commission shares the Subcommittee's concerns about deceptive concussion protection and other safety benefit claims for sports equipment. Claims that implicate serious health concerns

– especially those potentially affecting children and young adults – are always a high priority for the Commission," Ramirez said. "Given the dangers that concussions and other injuries pose for athletes, it is essential that advertising for products claiming safety benefits be truthful and substantiated. Using its existing authority, the Commission has been active in this area. For example, in 2012, the agency settled allegations that mouthguard manufacturer Brain-Pad and its president made false and unproven claims that Brain-Pad mouthguards reduced the risk of concussions. Following that case, the FTC sent warning letters to almost thirty sports equipment manufacturers and five retailers, advising them of the case and warning them that they also might be making deceptive concussion protection claims. The agency also investigated three major football helmet manufacturers – Riddell Sports, Schutt Sports, and Xenith – in connection with their claims that their helmets reduced the risk of concussions. In these matters, the staff closed the investigations without taking formal action, by which time all three companies had discontinued potentially deceptive claims from their advertising or had agreed to do so. H.R. 4460 would provide additional tools to protect consumers from such claims." (testimony)

Another witness was **Dr. Gregory O'Shanick, Medical Director of the Center for Neurorehabilitation Services in Richmond, Virginia.**

"The Youth Sports Concussion Act would help ensure that safety standards for sports equipment are based on the latest science and curb false advertising claims made by manufacturers to increase protective sports gear sales. An extensive National Academy of

Sciences report previously found a lack of scientific evidence that helmets and other protective devices designed for young athletes reduce concussion risk - yet some manufacturers continue to use false advertising claims that prevent athletes, parents and coaches from making informed safety decisions," Dr. O'Shanick said. "In 2012, the Federal Trade Commission (FTC) warned nearly 20 sports equipment manufacturers that they might be making deceptive concussion prevention claims, but the FTC's actions thus far have not deterred companies from making these claims. The Youth Sports Concussion Act would empower the FTC to seek civil penalties in such cases." (testimony)

The Youth Sports Concussion Act (bill) would help ensure that safety standards for sports equipment, including football helmets, are based on the latest science and curb false advertising claims made to increase protective sports gear sales. Sports are the second-leading cause of traumatic brain injuries for youth 15-24 years old, and athletes suffer up to 3.8 million concussions every year. An extensive National Academy of Sciences report, Sports-Related Concussions in Youth: Improving the Science, Changing the Culture, previously found that there is a lack of scientific evidence that helmets and other protective devices designed for young athletes reduce concussion risk — yet some manufacturers continue to use false advertising claims that prevent athletes, parents and coaches from making informed safety decisions.

In 2012, the Federal Trade Commission (FTC) warned nearly 20 sports equipment manufacturers that they might be making deceptive concussion prevention claims, but the FTC's actions thus far have not been an effective deterrent. The Youth Sports Concussion Act would empower the FTC to seek civil penalties in such cases.

Rep. Pascrell has been raising awareness of traumatic brain injury dangers and treatments for more than 15 years, including the House passage of his Concussion Treatment and Care Tools (ConTACT) Act, which provides for national protocols to be established for managing sports-related concussions. The ConTACT Act directs CDC to convene a conference of medical, athletic, and education stakeholders to establish model concussion management guidelines; and authorizes grants to states to establish, disseminate, and implement concussion management guidelines for school-sponsored sports and fund schools' implementation of baseline and post-concussion neuropsychological testing technologies. While the bill was blocked in the Senate, Congressman Pascrell was successful in urging CDC to establish the Pediatric Mild Traumatic Brain Injury Expert Panel, which is in the process of drafting concussion management guidelines that are expected in 2016.

Numerous sports, medical and consumer organizations have supported the Youth Sports Concussion Act, including:
American Academy of Neurology
American Academy of Pediatrics
Brain Injury Association of America
Brain Trauma Foundation
Cleveland Clinic
Consumer Federation of America
Consumers Union
Major League Baseball
Major League Baseball Players Association

Major League Soccer
Major League Soccer Players Union
National Association of State Head Injury
  Administrators
National Athletic Trainers' Association
National Basketball Association
National Collegiate Athletic Association
National Consumers League
National Federation of State High School Associations
National Football League
National Football League Players Association
National Hockey League
National Hockey League Players' Association
National Interscholastic Athletic Administrators
  Association
National Operating Committee on Standards for
  Athletic Equipment
Safe Kids Worldwide
United States Brain Injury Alliance
US Lacrosse
US Soccer Federation
USA Hockey
Xenith

1. According to those who provided testimony, the federal government investigated sports companies that sold protective gear purported to prevent head injuries. Why?

"OPENING STATEMENT OF THE HONORABLE FRED UPTON SUBCOMMITTEE ON OVERSIGHT AND INVESTIGATIONS HEARING ON 'CONCUSSIONS IN YOUTH SPORTS: EVALUATING PREVENTION AND RESEARCH,'" BY THE HONORABLE FRED UPTON, FROM THE US HOUSE OF REPRESENTATIVES, MAY 13, 2016

This hearing marks the second event of the committee's comprehensive review of concussions. We first had a roundtable discussion in March that highlighted not only the gaps in our scientific and medical understanding of these injuries but also the risks they pose to all members of society. These injuries occur not only on the field of play or in service to the nation, but also in the school yard, in auto accidents, or even something as simple as slipping on a patch of ice. They do not discriminate.

There are no easy answers when it comes to head trauma. It may take time for research to provide the concrete answers the public demands but that is not an excuse for inaction. There has been tremendous progress in the last decade but we can, and must, do more. And this must be a collective effort as no one individual, group, or organization can solve this public health challenge.

We are here today to examine what is being done to protect one the largest at-risk populations for concussions, youth athletes. Every year, in Michigan and across the country, tens of millions of children compete in youth sports. From community recreational teams to elite travel clubs, children have countless opportunities to engage in athletic competition. These activities provide tremendous benefits to our children, influencing their physical and psychological health, academic performance, and social well-being – both now and in the future.

Despite these benefits, with everything we see in the press about concussions and the long-term effects of head injuries, countless parents are asking themselves, is it safe for my child to play sports? This is a difficult question to answer. To start, we know relatively little about the prevalence, effects, and long-term outcomes of concussions or head injuries in pediatric populations, including youth sports. This group has been dramatically underrepresented in existing research. Do children respond differently than adults? How does the developing brain respond? Does it heal faster or does it create long-term effects? These are just a few of the many questions science simply cannot answer at this point.

In the absence of scientific answers, we look for opportunities to limit exposure to head injuries. Due to the nature of concussions, management of these injuries is difficult even in controlled settings such as pro sports where you have individual leagues with a limited number of teams and athletes. At the youth level, there are thousands of leagues, organizations, and clubs – making the challenge exponentially more difficult and harder to control. The adoption and enforcement of rules, policies, or education programs often depends on the commitment of individual leagues, teams, coaches, parents, and athletes.

Some progress has occurred in recent years as a number of leagues and organizations are taking steps to limit contact in practice and games. Others are conducting outreach and education to improve awareness and understanding for coaches, parents, and athletes. Whether these efforts are effective or go far enough remains a question and one that we should continue to evaluate. Collectively, however, these efforts reflect a growing shift in the culture of sports regarding concussions and head injuries. Today's discussion is an important step in the right direction.

1. According to Fred Upton, what can the government do to prevent brain injuries due to youths participating in high-contact sports in the absence of more in-depth scientific knowledge?

CHAPTER 3

WHAT THE COURTS SAY

The most famous court case involving contact sports and injuries associated with it is a massive lawsuit settled between former National Football League (NFL) players and the NFL itself.

Criticized by many for being too lenient on the NFL and for not doing enough to ensure the safety of future players, the controversy still lingers and the issue has become even more litigious.

In 2016, a lawyer representing retired NFL players filed an appeal in order to try and get the concussion settlement deal negated. This came only a few days after NFL executives admitted that football injuries can lead to chronic traumatic encephalopathy.

The attorney, Steven F. Molo, wants the appeals court to reject the deal because the settlement does not provide compensation for current or future players. In the one billion dollar settlement, the NFL only agreed to compensate players found to have the brain injury between 2006 and 2015.

Several more players have joined the appeal.

"The NFL's statements make clear that the NFL now accepts what science already knows: a 'direct' link exists between traumatic brain injury and CTE," Molo wrote in a letter that accompanied the appeal. "Given that, the settlement's failure to compensate present and future CTE is inexcusable."

But these are not the only lawsuits in the court system.

Some individuals are suing to make the games safer. Some are suing to hold sports leagues, coaches, or teams responsible. On the other end of the spectrum, some parents are suing so that their children can continue playing despite injury or in order to bypass any sort of safety protocol.

"YOUTH AND HIGH SCHOOL SPORTS CONCUSSION CASES: DO THEY SHOW THE LIMITS OF LITIGATION IN MAKING SPORTS SAFER?, BY DONALD C. COLLINS AND LINDSEY BARTON STRAUS, FROM MOMSTEAM

Major class action concussion litigation, which began with suits against the National Football League, NCAA, and NHL, reached the high school and youth level last year with the filing of a youth soccer lawsuit in California (Mehr

v. FIFA), and one challenging concussion management practices in high school football in Illinois (Pierscionek v. IHSA). In both cases, the defendants filed motions to dismiss. In July 2015, a federal court dismissed the youth soccer lawsuit. A decision from the Illinois state court on whether the high school football lawsuit should also be dismissed or proceed to trial is expected soon.

MEHR V. FIFA

In Mehr v. Federation Internationale De Football Association, a group of youth soccer players sued FIFA, the US Soccer Federation, the US Youth Soccer Association, the California Youth Soccer Association, US Club Soccer, and the American Youth Soccer Organization in the U.S. District Court for the Northern District of California. In their complaint, the plaintiffs claimed that FIFA and the youth soccer groups failed to adopt and enforce rules which would have reduced the risk and severity of concussions and brain injury allegedly the result of repetitive heading

The soccer players sought to force FIFA and the youth soccer groups to ban heading in soccer below age 17 (at the hearing on the motion to dismiss, plaintiffs' counsel for the first time suggested that they might only be seeking a complete ban for players under age 14 or that the number of times a player could hit the ball with his/her head be limited), relaxation of the rule allowing only three substitutions per game, and the creation of a massive medical monitoring fund for all past, present and future youth soccer players who may have suffered either a concussion or a sub-concussive hit (a group which would essentially include *every* youth soccer player other than those who never had contact with anybody and never headed a ball).

In a 46-page decision issued in July 2015, Judge Phyliss Hamilton granted the defendants' motions to dismiss. As to FIFA, Judge Hamilton based her dismissal on a finding that FIFA could not be sued in California, or what lawyers call a lack of personal jurisdiction. This lack of jurisdiction illustrates a difference between law and politics.

Under the law, a party cannot be forced to defend a lawsuit in the courts of a state (state or federal) unless it either has continuous and systematic contacts with the state sufficient to establish a physical "presence" in the state, or a three-prong test is met: (1) its activities in the state were such that it could reasonably anticipate being sued in the state; (2) the plaintiff's claims would not have arisen "but for" the defendant's activities in the state; and (3) the court's exercise of jurisdiction over the defendant is reasonable.

In Mehr, the court ruled that FIFA, as an association organized under Swiss law and with its principal place of business in Zurich, Switzerland, and with no office in California, was not sufficiently "at home" in California that it could be haled into a California court to defend a lawsuit.

Nor could the soccer players meet the three-prong test for limited jurisdiction. While the court found that allegations that FIFA had entered into various commercial arrangements or agreements in California might satisfy the first or "purposeful availment" prong, plaintiff fell short of alleging that, "but for" FIFA's activities in California, their claims - which were based on FIFA's alleged failure to change the Laws of the Game to require enactment of concussion management protocols, mandate substitution rules that allow for medical evaluation without penalty, and mandate limits on heading in practices and games by younger players - would not exist.

It was not enough to establish jurisdiction over FIFA, the court said, that it exerted "massive worldwide influence and regulation over all aspects of soccer, including in the United States and in California," that FIFA "engages in a broad swath of commercial activities in the U.S. and in California, strategically reinforcing its 'brand' and its primacy in the world of soccer and entrenching its influence," and that it "has extracted and continues to extract, massive sums of money from the U.S. and California, and has not contributed to protecting the safety of the youth players to which it markets and influences."

POLITICAL FOOTBALL

In other words, the court was saying, in so many words, that plaintiffs' lawsuit against FIFA was essentially based on *political,* not legal arguments, based on FIFA's control and influence over world soccer at all levels of the game, including at the lower levels of soccer, which have adopted rules that mirror FIFA's Laws of the Game.

From a political standpoint, the lawsuit made sense: because FIFA is responsible for all things soccer, there could be no more inviting target, politically, if the objective was to generate publicity and put public pressure on FIFA to change the Laws of the Game.

From a strictly legal standpoint, however, the lawsuit was doomed from the start: that, from its headquarters in Switzerland, FIFA exerts a tremendous sway over American youth soccer, is not the same as actually running youth leagues in California, and FIFA's strong influence over rules adopted by youth soccer organizations in California alone was not enough to make them subject to a court's jurisdiction.

We believe the court was correct in concluding that it lacked jurisdiction over FIFA. MomsTEAM readers who aren't lawyers might find the distinction between political sway and legal jurisdiction odd, but let's put the distinction differently. What if a MomsTEAM reader living New York, after suggesting a concussion management protocol that a MomsTeam reader in Minnesota adopted, got sued in Minnesota by a group of Minnesotans who thought that the New Yorker's program was flawed? The New Yorker would probably find it most unfair to be dragged into a Minnesota court, right? Well, the only difference between FIFA and the New Yorker is scale. In other words, just because FIFA's power makes it an inviting target of litigation doesn't change the law.

COMEDY OF ERRORS

While there was virtually nothing the plaintiffs' lawyers could have done to prevent dismissal of their claims against FIFA for lack of jurisdiction, the same, in our view, was not true with respect to the California youth soccer groups.

In contrast to the dismissal of the claims against FIFA on jurisdcictional grounds, the court dismissed the claims against the California youth soccer groups because of what can only be described as a comedy of pleading errors, including:

- failing to allege that any of the seven plaintiffs had actually suffered injury as an alleged result of any action or inaction by the California youth soccer groups. Only one had ever suffered a concussion, which was not caused by heading

the ball. Instead, they all simply pleaded a vari-
ation of a single allegation: that he/she was
at *increased risk* of latent brain injuries caused
by repeated head impacts or the accumulation
of concussive and/or subconcussive hits, and
therefore was in need of medical monitoring);
- picking as plaintiffs (and class representatives)
six individuals who were not currently playing
soccer and a seventh who did not allege that he
faced any threat of imminent harm that was not
purely speculative or hypothetical;
- naming as plaintiffs who were either over the
age of 17, and thus out of the age-range for
seeking modifications to rules governing youth
soccer, and under-17 plaintiffs who failed to
allege any imminent risk of injury traceable to
any California youth soccer defendant; and
- seeking an order altering the FIFA Laws of the
Game when the sole party with the power to
implement changes, the International Football
Association Board, was not joined in the lawsuit.

Not only was Mehr correctly dismissed on
jurisdictional and standing grounds, but Judge Hamilton
was correct in finding that the Complaint failed to state
facts sufficient to support negligence claims against the
California youth soccer defendants because it failed to
make a threshold showing that they owed plaintiffs a duty
of care. The reason was because they had no obligation
under the law to prevent risks inherent to playing the sport
of soccer (such as concussions), and absent from the
Complaint was any basis for imputing to any defendant a

legal duty to reduce the risks in the sport of soccer, or that any defendant took any action that *increased* the risks beyond those inherent in the sport of soccer.

The court also found, correctly in our view, that the plaintiffs had failed to plead facts showing that any act or omission by the defendants was a substantial factor in bringing about an injury suffered by plaintiff. Not only did the plaintiffs fail to allege facts that they suffered *any* injury - including a concussion - as a result of the defendants' negligence, but the court viewed the allegations of injury as "vague, conclusory, and entirely speculative, rather than concrete and particularized." (no doubt because the current state of the science allows for no more than that)

Finally, Judge Hamilton found that the defendant youth soccer organizations did not voluntarily assume a duty to adopt or enforce the consensus guidelines drafted by the various International Conferences on Concussion in Sport, nor had they specifically undertaken to take actions to eliminate risks inherent in the sport of soccer or to reduce the risk of injury from improper concussion management.

The court ultimately found that the soccer players' claims that FIFA and the youth soccer groups' rules were deficient were not claims that they took an action to increase the risk in the sport. The court was correct: failure to decrease the risks is not the same as taking an action to increase the risks, and one must increase the risks to be liable.

In short, the soccer players' attorney forgot three basic principles of negligence law every attorney learns in their first year of law school: that the plaintiff, in order to be entitled to relief, must suffer a concrete injury, that injury must be caused by the action or inaction of the defendant, and that the defendant owed the plaintiff a duty of care. Absent allegations that, if proven, would entitle a plaintiff to relief, the case cannot proceed to trial and must be dismissed. The federal district court in Mehr had little choice but to dismiss the soccer players' case.

APPLYING THE LAW

The dismissal by Judge Hamilton of the Mehr case teaches us a fundamental truth about the law: it can't be ignored in order to provide a forum for those dissatisfied with a private organization's rules. Rather, courts are a forum to provide remedies for injuries. Sometimes the remedy for the injury may be a change in a rule, so, in that respect, the players weren't completely out of line asking for change. The problem is that they - and, more importantly, their lawyers - chose a forum completely ill-suited for mounting a challenge to the Laws of the Game governing worldwide soccer. We'd be naive to pretend that there aren't political lawsuits, but even a political lawsuit has to honor the legal requirements of jurisdiction and injury. The soccer players' attorneys failed to meet this threshold standard.

PIERSCIONEK V. IHSA

In Pierscionek v. IHSA, a former Illinois high school football player is suing the Illinois High School Association in Illinois state court. (the original case was filed as Bukal v. IHSA, but was recaptioned after the original plaintiff, Daniel Bukai, dropped out of the case; for Don Collins' original thoughts on the case, shortly after it was filed, click here) [*Editor's note: hyperlinks can be found in the original article.*]

Some of the same flaws that led to the dismissal in <u>Mehr v. FIFA</u> could lead to dismissal in <u>Pierscionek</u> as well. As <u>Mehr</u> demonstrated, a plaintiff in a concussion class action has to do more than assert a claim on a hot button issue, and contend that the governing body of a sport hasn't done enough to protect athletes from harm. It is only human to feel sympathy for a former athlete suffering from the effects of one or more concussions or repeated impacts to the head. But sympathy alone is not enough. The requirements of the law still must be satisfied, whether one is suing the IHSA in an Illinois State court or suing FIFA and youth soccer groups in a California federal court.

The Illinois high school football case is unlikely to be dismissed on procedural grounds as was <u>Mehr</u>. Joe Siprut, the attorney for the Illinois football players, was far more careful than the youth soccer players' attorney in <u>Mehr</u>. The IHSA has claimed that Pierscionek's complaint is barred by the statute of limitations based on the date Pierscionek says he was injured, but the Complaint is only marginally late, and we believe a court will cut Pierscionek some slack, since he needed some time to realize that he was suffering from the after-effects of the concussion.

The Illinois football case may not have procedural problems, but it has some substantive problems. It may very well be dismissed before trial because, in our view, it simply doesn't state a claim under which the IHSA can be found liable, for much the same reasons as were cited by Judge Hamilton in dismissing <u>Mehr</u>, namely that a football player assumes the inherent risks of the game, so that, as long as the IHSA didn't take steps to make those inherent risks worse, it can't be found negligent. Concussions are clearly an inherent risk of the game, and the Complaint in <u>Pierscionek</u> doesn't allege that the IHSA made the inherent risk of concussions worse.

As much as Siprut wants a trial, if he can't state a claim, the Illinois football case will be dismissed before it gets that far. To his credit, Siprut realizes he has an assumption of risk problem, which he addresses by relying on the Illinois Protecting Our Student Athletes Act, 105 ILCS 5/10-20.54, which requires every Illinois school board to adopt a concussion policy which complies with the IHSA's policies and bylaws, and requires the IHSA to disseminate concussion educational materials to all school districts.

Siprut's problem is that he overplays his legal hand by erroneously claiming that the Act makes the IHSA the only group that can pass concussion regulation, and that the IHSA did not write sufficiently good rules. In truth, numerous entities can and do promulgate concussion management guidelines, including the National Federation of High Schools, whose rules the IHSA must follow. Further, every school district in Illinois, while required by the Protecting Our Student Athletes Act to adopt concussion policies, is free to enact its own rules, as long they meet the IHSA's minimum standards.

As a result, the Protecting Our Student Athletes Act has little legal significance, in effect codifying what was already the case: that IHSA member schools must follow IHSA rules; that the NFHS also writes rules that the IHSA must follow; and that IHSA schools can write regulations that are more strict than IHSA rules. It appears that, in enacting the Protecting Our Student Athletes Act, the Illinois legislature simply meant to highlight an important safety area and have local school boards actively declare that they were adhering to IHSA rules in this particular area. In more common vernacular, the Act really means that "schools have to follow IHSA rules, and we really mean it and we're going to make the schools say so because this is really, really important to us in the Illinois legislature ... so there."

Not surprisingly, the IHSA doesn't quibble with Siprut's error; instead, it uses it to its advantage by arguing that the it can't be found to have acted negligently because it disseminated educational material as required by the Act, and can't be found liable for negligent rulemaking when it is the purview of the Illinois legislature to enact rules.

Stripped of his claim that the Act makes the IHSA solely responsible for enacting rules governing concussion management, Siprut faces the same problem that the attorney for the youth soccer players faced in <u>Mehr</u>: he must find a way to show that the IHSA's concussion regulations made the inherent risks of football *worse*.

In arguing for dismissal, the IHSA, however, goes even further than the youth soccer governing bodies in <u>Mehr</u>. The IHSA argues that it can't be negligent under the contact sports exception, which says that a player in a sport or activity can't be found negligent where he or she commits an act which is a penalty, foul or harmful act, but is an act that every reasonable person who plays the sport expects to happen and knows that they will have to deal with. In layman's terms, I may be negligent when I commit a personal foul in a basketball game by smacking you in the eye while trying to block your shot, but everybody who plays basketball knows that there's a chance that they'll get poked in the eye during the game. Once in a very rare blue moon, some guy is going to get a detached retina. He doesn't get to sue me because he's the one in a billion guy. The "contact sports exception" applies.

The IHSA may well be correct in relying on the contact sports exception. The exception is supposed to protect *players* who injure *other players* in the normal course of play. But in a 2008 case, Karas v. Strevell, the Illinois Supreme Court extended the contact sports exception to protect organizations. Interestingly, Karas relies upon a 2003 California Supreme Court case called Kahn v. East Side Union High Schl. District, which is a bit odd, because Kahn ruled that coaches can only be liable if they are grossly negligent when engaged in coaching actions, which are a lot broader than playing actions, and the logic of protecting a coach is different than the logic of protecting a player from the ramifications of actions he takes while playing. Yes, Karas misses the point, but Karas is the law in Illinois and it may very well win the case for the IHSA.

The Illinois football case will probably be dismissed and never get to trial. It will either be dismissed because the IHSA did not make the inherent risks of play any worse or it will be dismissed under the Illinois expansion of the contact sports exception.

WHAT COMES NEXT?

The concussion class action litigations against the National Football League and NCAA resulted in highly publicized settlements, so what are the chances that the high school football and youth soccer class actions will go that route? Two things to note:

First, the NFL and NCAA cases were settled on terms that most observers feel were highly favorable to the defendants. In fact, the NCAA's initial concussion settlement in Arrington v. NCAA was rejected by a US District judge because it didn't sufficiently address the needs of the class of plaintiffs, as was the case in the NFL concussion lawsuit as well.

Second, that a professional sports league and the governing body for college sports settled don't necessarily provide a template for suits involving high school or youth athletes. Unfortunately, they probably led some attorneys to think that, if they filed lawsuits, the governing bodies for sports at those levels would be quick to settle as well. That hasn't happened. Clearly, Mehr and Pierscionek are more a product of wishful thinking by the plaintiffs' attorneys than sound cases on the actual merits.

Besides, youth sports and high school leagues don't have the deep pockets possessed by the N.F.L. and the NCAA (which is undoubtedly one of the reasons the plaintiffs in Mehr sued FIFA, which *does* have deep pockets), so they are much less likely to see a monetary settlement involving expensive medical monitoring programs, as sought by the plaintiffs in Mehr and Pierscionek, as something they could afford.

Undoubtedly, the plaintiff personal injury bar (what we lawyers call tort lawyers) will learn from their mistakes in Mehr and Pierscionek. They'll stop trying to bring big cases to challenge and change sports' governing bodies' rules, and instead target individual schools, school districts and leagues for not enforcing the rules that *do* exist and for egregious departures from best safety practices. A number of schools and districts may even settle for some of the remedies that the sports governing bodies found objectionable in Mehr and Pierscionek.

Finally, it should be noted that the NCAA and NFL concussion settlements are not going to be the end of concussion litigation involving pro and college sports. A suit against the NHL is ongoing, a significant number of former NFL players have opted out of the settlement reached between the NFL and some are opting out of the NCAA settlement as well.

If those plaintiffs, through the discovery process, obtain documents showing that the NCAA or a professional sports league had actual knowledge of the long-term risks of concussions, then we could very well see juries return huge verdicts which could change the face of sports in the way the huge punitive damage awards against Ford Motor Company (Pinto) and General Motors (Corvair) in the 60's and 70's did for car safety by showing that athletes may assume the inherent risks of play, but the law may find that they do not assume risks that won't manifest for decades where a sports governing body knew about those risks and hid them. (although not out of the realm of possibility, the likelihood that organizations overseeing sports at the youth and high school level possess those kind of documents is remote)

The bottom line: the NFL, NCAA, NHL cases and Mehr and Pierscionek aren't the beginning of the end for concussion litigation, they are likely just the end of the beginning.

1. What are some reasons the author of this article states that class actions against youth sports organizations will potentially be different than these court cases against professional sports organizations like the NFL or the Fédération Internationale de Football Association (FIFA)?

"WHERE IS SPORTS CONCUSSION LITIGATION HEADED?," BY STEVEN M. SELLERS, FROM *CLASS ACTION LITIGATION REPORT*, FEBRUARY 19, 2016

Feb. 18 — Concussion litigation—and the brain injury science that underlies it—is trickling from the ranks of professional athletes to amateur and youth players, and that may create an expanding pool of future plaintiffs and new legal challenges for defendants, lawyers and academics tell Bloomberg BNA.

Repetitive head trauma often begins in youth sports, and the impact on young brains may be the key to future sports concussion litigation, the lawyers say. Developments in chronic brain injury diagnosis may also raise the odds of suits by youth and adult amateur players against equipment manufacturers, schools and non-profit sports leagues.

Predicted diagnostic tools that will detect chronic traumatic encephalopathy in living athletes—a chronic degenerative disease found in the brains of some deceased NFL and NHL players—may change the litigation calculus significantly, the lawyers add.

But how will recent class action concussion settlements with the National Football League and the National Collegiate Athletics Association frame future sports concussion litigation?

Paul Anderson, a plaintiff's lawyer with The Klamann Law Firm in Kansas City, Mo., who also blogs on concussion litigation, told Bloomberg BNA Feb. 12 he sees a "tidal wave" of litigation ahead as a result of the settlements.

"It's had an impact at all levels, starting with the NFL and then shortly thereafter the NCAA, and now you're seeing it in high school and peewee," said Anderson. "And it's not just limited to football—it's all sports."

Others interviewed for this report agreed.

"Whenever one corporate entity pays money to a claimant, more claims follow," Mark Granger, of Granger Legal Consulting, Inc., in Schroon Lake, N.Y., who chairs the Sports and Fitness Industry Association's Legal Task Force, told Bloomberg BNA Feb. 14 in an e-mail.

"We expect concussion litigation to become a significant new field of law, potentially involving regular class action suits and mirroring what once existed with asbestos, cigarettes, and lead paint," according to Granger, formerly with Morrison Mahoney's Boston office, whose clients have included Easton Sports, Franklin Sports and Reebok.

Granger said he wasn't speaking on behalf of those or other sports industry clients.

NFL, NCAA SETTLEMENTS SET STAGE

Lawyers for former players who sued the NFL say the $675 million uncapped class settlement already has risen to $1 billion, and may increase "exponentially" if currently asymptomatic players develop symptoms at a higher rate than predicted *(In re Nat'l Football League Players' Concussion Injury Litig.,* 2015 BL 114599, E.D. Pa., MDL No. 2323, final settlement approved 4/22/15).

Another, tentatively approved, $75 million class settlement with the NCAA for a class comprised of all current and former student-athletes may invite further litigation because athletes retain the ability to bring tort claims against the NCAA or its member institutions for a future brain injury diagnosis (*In re Nat'l. Collegiate Athletic Ass'n Student-Athlete Concussion Litig.,* N.D. Ill., MDL No. 2492, preliminary class settlement approved 1/26/16).

Yet another federal multidistrict litigation is pending over the concussion injury claims of former National Hockey League players (*In re Nat'l Hockey League Players' Concussion Injury Litig.,* D. Minn., No. 14-md-02251, filed, 8/19/14).

But medical science may be the strongest barometer for future concussions-related cases—a conclusion evident in the NFL litigation itself.

FOCUS ON YOUTH CONCUSSIONS?

"The science could determine really that all that matters for developing CTE is how many hits you take before your eighteenth birthday," Paul Clement, a lawyer for the NFL, told the U.S. Court of Appeals for the Third Circuit last November in oral argument of an appeal by objectors who are challenging the class settlement as insufficient (*In re Nat'l Football League Players' Concussion Injury Litig.*, 3d Cir., No. 15-2304, oral argument, 11/19/15)

Clement is with the Bancroft law firm in Washington.

CTE, found in the brains of some deceased NFL players, currently may only be diagnosed post-mortem. That may soon change, however, according to Dr. Robert Stern, a professor of neurology, neurosurgery, anatomy and neurobiology at Boston University School of Medicine, Boston, Mass.

"Based on the scientific and medical literature, my own first-hand knowledge of the current state of the scientific field, and on my own research, I am confident that within the next five to ten years there will be highly accurate, clinically accepted, and FDA-approved methods to diagnose CTE during life," Stern said in a declaration filed in the NFL litigation.

Anderson said the tentative NCAA settlement alone will affect as many as 4.4 million student-athletes, some of whom may learn they have CTE in a future test.

"I think the NCAA settlement is going to trigger a tidal wave of litigation," said Anderson. "I can't believe the NCAA agreed to it. It's going to allow [players] to sue in the future on a diagnosis of CTE in the living."

"Fighting the science is going to be very difficult on the part of the NCAA because it was their settlement that allowed the diagnosis of CTE," said Anderson. "That settlement's going to go on for the next 50 years, so we're looking at a half-century of CTE litigation to come."

"Effective CTE diagnoses on living persons will change the landscape of litigation dramatically," Paul Haagen, a professor at Duke University Law School,

Durham, N.C., and director of its Center for Sports Law and Policy, told Bloomberg BNA Feb. 11.

"As the risks involved in playing these sports become better understood, the arguments for assumption of risk by the athletes—and their parents/guardians—will be stronger," Haagen said in an e-mail. "Because of the progressive nature of CTE, the arguments related to the onset of the disease are more powerful."

Potential streams of new CTE litigation will also multiply because of the notoriety of the NFL and NCAA settlements, Douglas Abrams, a professor at the University of Missouri School of Law, Columbia, Mo., told Bloomberg BNA Feb. 12.

"When the NFL does something, or the NCAA does something, the media notices and people notice," said Abrams, who writes extensively on legal and regulatory issues in youth sports concussions. "The fact that the litigation is happening in these high-profile organiza-tions is going to filter down to the youth league and high school levels and produce concussion litigation there, as well."

Those leagues include an estimated 30 to 45 million children and adolescents who participate in non-scho-lastic sports, and more than seven million athletes in the U.S. who compete in high school sports each year, according to a recent study of the incidence of youth sports concussions.

CASES TO WATCH

One indication of the trend may be found in tort suits filed against sports leagues by the parents of youths who suf-fered brain or spinal injuries in sports.

One California case cited by Abrams involves claims by the parents of a quadriplegic youth football player that Pop Warner league coaches trained their son to tackle with his helmet, increasing the likelihood of severe injury (*Dixon v. Pop Warner Little Scholars, Inc.*, Cal. Super. Ct., No. BC526842, filed, 11/5/13).

The case was recently resolved in a confidential settlement for an undisclosed amount.

Abrams added that similar scenarios may play out in other cases because of some distinct differences between high-level leagues and non-profit youth leagues and schools.

"Most youth leagues and high schools do not have certified trainers on the sidelines; they're too expensive," Abrams said. "So a lot of the burden falls on coaches."

Another pending case, Anderson said, is *Pyka v. Pop Warner Little Scholars, Inc.*, W.D. Wis., No. 15-cv-00057, filed 1/5/15, in which the parents of Joseph Chernach allege in part that their son's suicide was the result of repeated concussions and the league's failure to warn of the dangers of youth football.

Abrams said individual cases like these are sure to be on the rise in the future. But Granger, of the Sports and Fitness Industry Association, said, however, that it is "dubious" that class claims like those in the professional league MDLs will spread—as long as medical causation remains an issue.

"The NFL, NHL, and NCAA cases are based on alleged withholding [of] information from athletes and their families," said Granger. "These claims really don't exist for individual schools and not-for-profit leagues. Class claims against such defendants are not likely to be successful."

HELMET MANUFACTURERS ON GUARD?

Helmet manufacturers—also in the path of future concussion litigation—have taken steps to enhance the protective qualities of helmets and to detect on-field head impacts, but it's not clear helmets can prevent concussions, as opposed to skull fractures.

"The reality is that the helmet isn't going to be the answer because you can't stop the brain from rattling around in the skull," said Anderson. "It's just a matter of physics and science."

Riddell, Inc., a major manufacturer of football helmets, won a jury verdict in 2014 over allegations that a defectively designed helmet caused a high school player to suffer brain damage (*Acuna v. Riddell Sports, Inc.*, Cal. Super. Ct., No. LC090924, verdict entered, 3/20/14).

Observers suggested the verdict was based, in part, on the notion that jurors are receptive to arguments that athletes in contact sports assume the risk of injury.

"The liability of helmet and other equipment manufacturers is based both on faulty design and failure to warn," Haagen said. "In the future, it will depend a lot on how equipment manufacturers market their products and how effective they are at warning of risks."

William Staar, of Morrison Mahoney's Manchester, N.H. office, told Bloomberg BNA Feb. 14 in an e-mail that helmets are a part of player safety, but aren't designed to prevent concussions.

"Helmets were created and designed to prevent severe head trauma, e.g., skull fractures, subdural hematomas, and cerebral hemorrhage," said Staar, who advises the sporting goods industry and is also, like

Granger, a member of the Sports and Fitness Industry Association's Legal Task Force. "They have done this very effectively for decades. They were not designed and, to date, have not been successful in preventing concussions," said Staar.

"Helmets are, at best, only part of the solution to head trauma," Staar said. "Coaching, education of athletes, training, rulemaking, and better rule enforcement can and does reduce brain injury."

1. What do you think about this trend in court cases? Will such court cases help to protect future generations of student athletes participating in high-contact sports? Or are they just additional litigation in our already overly litigious society?

"SPECIAL REPORT: COMBATING CONCUSSIONS IN HIGH SCHOOL SPORTS," BY SEAN PEICK, FROM *CRONKITE NEWS*, MAY 6, 2013

PHOENIX – Mary Shannon suffered her first concussion during North High School soccer tryouts in 2011, colliding with the goalie and hitting her head on the ground.

Under a state law signed earlier that year, she had to receive written medical clearance to return to the field. That took a month.

After a collision with an opposing player left her with a second concussion earlier this year, Shannon decided that was enough. Having learned about the dangers of concussions and with encouragement from her parents, she quit, deciding to limit her involvement to refereeing and helping the team in other ways.

"Yes it's a big part of my life, and yes, I love it, but I can still participate in it without having to put myself in the danger of getting another concussion or some other injury," she said.

In Arizona, about 7,000 high school athletes suffer concussions each year, according to research by A.T. Still University in Mesa. While football justifiably gets most of the attention, concussions are a threat in any high school sport.

A 2011 state law requires that high school athletes be removed from play if a concussion is even suspected and then receive written clearance to return from a medical professional like a physician or athletic trainer.

The law also called for concussion-education programs for coaches, students and parents. This led to the Arizona Interscholastic Association requiring every high school athlete in Arizona to complete Barrow Brainbook, interactive online training developed in part by Barrow Neurological Institute at St. Joseph's Hospital and Medical Center.

But the effort didn't end with a law. Medical professionals, advocates and others have since offered free baseline cognitive testing, known as ImPACT, that helps measure the effects of concussions and established a network of concussion experts that athletic trainers can consult via telemedicine.

Soon, a voluntary registry created by Barrow and A.T. Still will allow high schools to report concussions to researchers looking to improve the safety of athletes.

Dr. Javier Cardenas, a child neurologist at the Barrow Neurological Institute, said Arizona's approach to concussions is "really the most comprehensive program like it in the country and likely the world."

Sen. Rich Crandall, R-Mesa, who shepherded Arizona's law through the Legislature, said that in the end keeping athletes safe comes down to students, parents and coaches recognizing the symptoms and keeping athletes with concussions off the field.

"If those three are on board, we're going to be able to make a difference in Arizona," he said.

ARIZONA'S LAW

When the National Football League approached him about following a Washington state law on concussions, Crandall said the time seemed right for Arizona.

"We're a big high school football state," Crandall said. "We're not Texas, but still, it's a big deal."

In the process of creating the legislation, Crandall said, he and advocates found that parents can be a barrier to acting in the best interests of an injured student athlete. As an example, he described a scenario in which a student is being considered for an athletic scholarship.

"The coach is saying, 'No, let's pull him out,' and the parent's saying, 'No, you don't get it. My boy needs to perform in front of these coaches, these scouts,'" Crandall said.

Signed by Gov. Jan Brewer, the law established a protocol that goes into effect when a high school athlete suffers what's even suspected of being a concussion. The athlete is immediately removed from play by either the coach, a referee or other official, a licensed health care provider or the athlete's parent.

If the athlete is examined by a licensed health care provider and a concussion is ruled out, he or she may return to play the same day. Otherwise, the athlete cannot return before receiving written clearance from a health care provider defined by the law as a physician, a physician assistant, a nurse practitioner or an athletic trainer.

The law also requires student athletes and their parents to sign a form acknowledging they have reviewed the risks and symptoms of concussions.

It's modeled on Washington state's 2009 Zackery Lystedt Law, named after a boy who suffered a brain injury in 2006 after returning to a middle school football game following a concussion.

As of late April, 47 states and Washington, D.C., had enacted youth concussion laws, most of them based on the Lystedt Law.

Dr. John Parsons, an associate professor and director of the athletic training program at A.T. Still University, said that the narrow definition of who can clear an athlete to return to competition sets Arizona's law apart. Laws in Washington and other states refer generally to health care providers, he said.

Parsons said the most common criticism of high school concussion laws is that there are no punishments for not following them.

"It's more or less honors policy, and you hope that the law compels them to be compliant," he said.

Crandall said the law doesn't need punishments to be effective.

"The fear for a school district would be somebody filing a suit for breaking the law," he said. "You don't have to have punitive penalties when that's kind of overarching from everybody. A coach puts a kid back in with a concussion and a parent sues – that's the last thing any school district wants."

The Arizona Interscholastic Association, an independent body that oversees high school athletics, doesn't track whether individual athletes or coaches have completed concussion training. It instead relies on schools, coaches, parents and others to report violations of its bylaws.

Chuck Schmidt, assistant executive director and chief operating officer of the AIA, said that if a complaint comes in the organization will look into it. But anything more than that just isn't feasible, he said.

"We don't have an NCAA budget in order to create that enforcement," he said. "But I think we do a fantastic job of utilizing our resources effectively and efficiently in the cases where we need to look into something and determine if it's a bylaw violation – be it from concussion to recruiting."

Sanctions vary depending on the nature of the violation, Schmidt said.

For example, he noted, Veritas Prep Academy in Phoenix recently reported a violation involving a boys basketball player who hadn't completed Brainbook. The AIA accepted the school's decision to forfeit games in which the player appeared and create procedures to guard against such an oversight.

BEYOND THE LAW

The day before she sustained her first concussion and pulled herself out of soccer tryouts, Mary Shannon had completed Barrow Brainbook.

"The symptoms were fresh in my mind," she said.

That's precisely what Dr. Javier Cardenas envisioned when he and others at Barrow helped create the online course in collaboration with the AIA, the Arizona Cardinals and A.T. Still. Since 2011, more than 150,000 students have completed it.

Cardenas said that Brainbook, which is designed to resemble a social media site, is unprecedented in the U.S.

"There is not a single state that provides athlete-specific, athlete-directed concussion education," he said. "We developed it because the CDC provides concussion education to coaches, to health care providers, to parents – but nothing directed at the athletes."

August 2012 saw the launch of the Barrow Concussion Network. One of the program's partnerships was with Dick's Sporting Goods and the ImPACT cognitive test to provided free baseline concussion testing for all AIA-member schools that don't offer the ImPACT test on their own. About 2,000 students took part this school year, a number Cardenas said was low because of late attempts at getting the word out.

The goal for next school year is 10,000 to 20,000 students, he said.

Another initiative from the Barrow Concussion Network allows athletic trainers across the state to consult via telemedicine with concussion experts in Phoenix on diagnoses and concussion management.

111

This fall, the network plans to launch what researchers hope turns into a detailed registry of all concussions in Arizona high school sports.

"The registry project is one that we initially came up with to really try and capture the number of concussions in Arizona and what happens to those student athletes," said Dr. Tamara McLeod, the John P. Wood, D.O., Endowed Chair for Sports Medicine and a professor in the Athletic Training Program at A.T. Still.

The purpose of the registry isn't merely tracking the number of concussions but collecting information on continuity of care and symptoms in concussion patients.

"We want to know more than the raw numbers," Cardenas said. "We want to know how people are actually being treated and how they're recovering."

The research is voluntary; although each event is reported by a particular school, if an athlete opts not to participate, the information will be wiped from the log.

If the athlete chooses to participate, he or she will provide information on their continuing care and symptoms.

Massachusetts is the only state that requires schools to report concussions. The regulations, which apply to public schools and members of the Massachusetts Interscholastic Athletic Association, require an annual accounting of head injuries and suspected concussions.

Paul Wetzel, spokesman for the MIAA, said the requirement is a research tool.

"There is not a lot of clinically gathered or anecdotally gathered data on concussions in high school sports," he said.

RESPONSIBILITY

When Mary Shannon sustained her second concussion in January, she wasn't knocked out, stumbling around or otherwise displaying symptoms that would have made it immediately obvious that she had a concussion.

"If I hadn't have pulled myself out, nobody would have pulled me out," she said. "It was kind of like, he (the coach) said, 'Are you OK?' and I said, 'I don't think so.'

"But if I had said I was OK, I probably would have been in the game."

Despite the requirements to remove athletes from play at even the hint of a concussion and to only return those who have received written clearance from a health care provider, medical professionals and others say that those aren't foolproof.

Dr. Ben Bobrow, the medical director for the Arizona Department of Health Services Bureau of EMS and Trauma System, said he suspects that athletes commonly minimize concussion symptoms. While severe concussions result in symptoms such as confusion, memory problems, a lack of muscle coordination known as ataxia and loss of consciousness, lesser concussions can result in minor symptoms such as headaches and dizziness that are much easier to hide.

"If you think about kids on the sideline or in a game, they want to play, they want to be in the game, they don't want to let on that they have some kind of problem," he said.

Chris White, head athletic trainer at Brophy College Preparatory in Phoenix, said that coaches play a crucial role because they can make sure athletes who may have suffered concussions don't return to play. But he said that the ultimate responsibility doesn't rest with any one group.

"It's a real team effort, and when you have a deficiency anywhere, it's a problem," White said.

Mattie Cummins, program director and former executive director of the Brain Injury Alliance of Arizona, said that the student and his or her parents can either help or hinder when an athlete has symptoms of a concussion.

"It's the parents and the kid who see behaviors or they feel behaviors after the game ends, when they go home, when they go to school," she said. "It's that parent or kid that has the control."

Many parents have been brought up to consider concussions "a bop on the head," she said, making it vital to make sure they know just how far-reaching the effects can be.

"The message that we're focusing on with parents is this concussion can affect their (the athlete's) world tomorrow," she said. "It can affect their world at 22. It can affect their world at 23, when they're out getting a job, when the sports is over. And really, it's not about today, it's about the rest of their lives."

THE FUTURE

While concussion research has made strides in recent years, including evidence linking concussions to cognitive and behavioral problems as well as depression and suicide, Bobrow with the Arizona Department of Health Services said that there is still much more that can be done.

"It's actually kind of a black box for us right now, we don't actually know how severe it is," he said. "Or, you know, we know a little about how many head injuries you can have before you have a big problem, and it's likely different for different people."

Schmidt said that the AIA updates its bylaws as often as necessary based on developments in preventing and responding to concussions.

"That's the primary goal of the AIA, to ensure the safety and health of our kids," Schmidt said.

On April 15, the AIA Executive Board approved a rule restricting the amount of time teams can practice full-contact while wearing pads. It's aimed at minimizing the risk of concussions and other injuries.

Crandall said Arizona law likely will remain as is for the foreseeable future but eventually will expand, just as the rules of football have changed over time to keep players safe.

"It's going to evolve, for sure," he said.

1. What should be the responsibility of the states in regard to minimizing risks for student athletes and what should be the responsibility of the federal government or individual leagues?

CHAPTER 4

WHAT ADVOCATES AND ADVOCACY GROUPS SAY

T hese last few years there has been a lot of talk, legal wrangling, research, and admissions concerning the dangers of young people and adults alike playing high-contact sports. While the rhetoric has been strong on both sides of the issue, there are some who have taken it upon themselves to not only advocate for safer sports but who are doing something about it.

One such organization is the fledgling Grand Prairie Youth Football Association in Grand Prairie, Texas. League administrators teamed up with representatives from the MomsTEAM Institute of Youth Sports Safety—in conjunction with the UNICEF International Safeguards of Children in Sports project—to hold a league-wide seminar on ways to keep enjoying the great sport of football but to also make it a safe and enjoyable experience.

Some of the steps the new league implemented was to establish a comprehensive emergency plan, learn the "heads up" tackling techniques, and limit the amount of physical contact that takes place during practice. Of course, critics complain that the lack of physical contact during practice results in poor tackling habits that can lead to more injuries.

It's a topic that is far from resolved, although advocates are working hard to make the playing field safer for student athletes in any way they can.

"TESTIMONY FOR PUBLIC HEARING 'CONCUSSIONS IN YOUTH SPORTS: EVALUATING PREVENTION AND RESEARCH,'" BY KAREN KINZLE ZEGEL, IN FRONT OF THE US HOUSE OF REPRESENTATIVES ENERGY AND COMMERCE COMMITTEE AND THE OVERSIGHT AND INVESTIGATIONS SUBCOMMITTEE, MAY 13, 2016

Thank you Energy and Commerce Committee members and particularly Representative Murphy for allowing me to speak to this hearing today. I consider it an honor and a privilege to represent the millions of children that are in harms way as we debate their future health and wellbeing.

I am not a doctor or scientist. But I have experience. I have lived with and loved a person struggling with the disease Chronic Traumatic Encephalopathy, CTE. I have seen close-up the transformation of a beautiful, bright, energetic, loving young man into a reclusive, paranoid, depressed and angry person. It is heartbreaking.

My son Patrick Risha was a hometown hero in high school football. He grew up in an area that measured the worth of a man by his prowess and heart on the football field. He started just south of Pittsburgh with the Elizabeth Forward youth leagues when he was ten years old. He was not gifted with size or speed but nonetheless worked hard to become a great player, and through that achieved his dream to go to an Ivy League school. It is that work ethic and perseverance in a collision sport that ultimately killed him. Patrick took his own life at the age of 32.... But actually we have come to learn CTE took his life.

Patrick never played in the NFL. Patrick was like millions of children before and after him that just played for success in life. But throughout high school, prep school and Dartmouth College, our sweet, tough, young running back received enough subconcussive blows to his head to essentially seal his fate. When he died, a newscaster friend of the family suggested he might have CTE. I had never heard of CTE before. I had heard about NFL players having brain issues but never dreamed it could have an effect at the level of a college player. When Patrick's autopsy revealed he had widespread CTE I was in shock and horror. How many other players like Patrick are there out there? How many other families are dealing with a loved one gradually coming unwired and have no clue what is happening? Not every grieving family has a newscaster friend saying the words CTE. For the sake of American families this has to change.....and we are grateful this committee is conducting this hearing to learn more about the disease and the impact on families and on our society.

People need to know that this disease is out there. That it can occur in youth and high school and college levels of collision sports. Families need to know what the symptoms are and how to address the disease. This has been hidden in plain sight for much too long. It was this realization that prompted our family and friends and the support of my husband, to form the Patrick Risha CTE Awareness Foundation and the website StopCTE.org. Sadly, I am not the only grieving loved one on this crusade. In March for Brain Injury Awareness Day here in the House twelve families were represented that lost loved ones to brain trauma and disease. Paul Bright, Eric Pelly, Daniel Brett and Joseph Chernach only played football up to the high school level. Their moms and other families of CTE victims formed the Save Your Brain Campaign to bring attention to the need for protecting children in sports. Together with many other families (as the numbers grow), we will be returning to DC until we are sure that children are protected and safe.

No family wants their child to suffer with a disease that causes them to lose their mind slowly and with such anxiety and loneliness. Yet everyday parents are signing their kids up for youth collision sports. Our "Steelers Country" area in Pennsylvania supports a television show called "Friday Night Tykes" with young children bashing heads on national television. These parents don't understand the horror that may face their child or they would not participate.

Since Roman times MEN have fought in arenas for sport and entertainment. Yet somehow we seem to have evolved to the point where we are now willing to put children into arenas and tackle each other for sport. We put them in the equivalent of cheap Halloween costumes and we ask them to be tough little warriors. We did it.

And we were so proud when Patrick carried his team to victory. Sadly we lost a gifted young man before he ever had a chance to live his life. And gifted children all over this land are winning battles on the sports fields but sadly losing their chances for a happy, healthy, productive life.

If I had known the collisions my son endured were slowly killing him, I would have stopped it. Any parent would who knows the truth would stop it. Parents need to be told the truth. Parents need to know:

- That 32% of amateur athletes in collision sports were found to have had CTE post mortem.
- Parents need to know that helmets and sports equipment are unregulated and may even add to the likelihood of brain trauma in children.
- Parents need to know that athletes that receive repetitive brain trauma before the age of 12 have significant changes in physiology, operations, and structure of the brain. So even if a child never gets CTE, he/she may still have done irreparable damage to the brain. Human brains are still developing until the age of 18 and sub-concussive blows to the head cause white matter changes, axon changes, and blood vessel changes, and these changes can be permanent.

  Parents need to know that recognizing a concussion in a child is often very challenging. Kids won't even tell you when they are tired, let alone tell you if they have vision problems, sensitivity to noise, trouble concentrating, or feel emotionally changed.

- Parents need to know that their child can develop CTE without ever receiving a concussion.
- Parents need to know that less that half of youth football coaches are well trained in concussion management. Coaches do know that the team plays better when the best players are on the field. So where is the incentive in the heat of competition to do the right thing at the right time?

Our Foundation created a brochure, "Flag Until 14" to help parents understand the key issues of CTE. We intend to place these brochures in every pediatrician office in the country. We have reached 62 practices so far. We have much more work to do.

Heading the ball has recently been eliminated from youth soccer. Checking in hockey has been eliminated in youth leagues. Football needs to institute "Flag until 14", at the very least. (We would prefer Flag Until 50) Now the information is out there. Now we need to pay attention to it. At the very least, we need to protect those precious little brains. Right now children need us to help protect them.

There are those out there who would prefer parents didn't know about CTE. They will obfuscate the issue with unreasoned arguments. We've heard a few like "you can get a concussion riding a bike" or "you're turning our warriors into pansies" or "do you want them to sit and play video games for the rest of their lives?" When you've lost your son to CTE, and you understand how it is caused, these arguments are insulting, and almost evil. So for now, please let's just help protect the kids.

And what about the men and women who already have CTE? We believe that this silent epidemic may be playing out in millions of homes across this land. Families are burying loved ones all over this country thinking they died from suicide, drug addictions, PTSD, depression, ADHD, and irrational behaviors. Thinking that somehow something happened to change the person they loved, and feeling somehow that they failed them. Very few are linking these deaths to CTE.....

Maybe they don't know to ask. Maybe a doctor misdiagnosed the patient. Maybe the coroner is rushing to judgment. Maybe the behaviors in their loved ones changed so slowly that no one is linking it to previous military or sports history from so many years ago. Whatever the reasons, the silent epidemic continues. And we believe the magnitude of this horrific disease has yet to be discovered. Gunplay and murders are in the news every evening, and we always wonder how many of the perpetrators played collision sports or served in the military. Just as many suicides are NOT reported every evening because of the stigma attached to suicide. We muffle the fact that a reported 22 veterans a day commit suicide, and that suicides exceed homicides every year.

What also continues? Beautiful children are being placed in harms way through collision sports everyday. Families and loved ones are in turmoil. People are losing their lives. Mental health practices, drug addiction facilities, and suicide centers are on overload. Lawyers are filing lawsuits all over the place. Insurances are going up.

We also have some suggestions for better insight, research and ultimately help for victims and their families:

- The CDC death certificate needs to have a box to check if the victim played a collision sport, and in turn the possibility for death from CTE should be noted on the death certificate.
- The jails nation wide should do a study on how many inmates played a collision sport or were in the military. Rehab facilities should do the same.
- Mental health providers need trained to recognize and treat CTE
- No school or organization should field a collision sports team without a certified medical specialist on the field.

In my sons memory, we set our mission to increase awareness of the insidious disease, CTE, and to help parents make informed decisions about the safety and welfare of our children, and to provide a resource to promote greater understanding of the challenge we face dealing with this silent epidemic. This is a human tragedy of immense proportions, but we are small and need the help of everyone in the room and in the halls of Congress.

After we are done hearing everyone's testimony today we will know that children are in danger and need our help and that families are in crisis. Parents are receiving conflicting data and just don't know. We can't be the only doomsday placard holder in the street. Every person in this room now has the duty to save these children and families. CTE is 100% preventable. To do anything else is to be complicit to the problem and more families will suffer the pain we personally endure every day.

Thank you so much for the opportunity to be a voice for children.

1. This advocate states that, since many cases of CTE may go undiagnosed, those who commit crimes or suicide may have done so due to undiagnosed CTE. What do you think about this?

2. An argument often used against such advocates by parents is that new sports regulations will turn their children, and especially their sons, into "pansies." Do you think this is a valid argument? Why or why not?

"TESTIMONY FOR PUBLIC HEARING 'CONCUSSIONS IN YOUTH SPORTS: EVALUATING PREVENTION AND RESEARCH,'" BY KELLI JANZ, IN FRONT OF THE US HOUSE OF REPRESENTATIVES ENERGY AND COMMERCE COMMITTEE AND THE OVERSIGHT AND INVESTIGATIONS SUBCOMMITTEE, MAY 13, 2016

Chairman Murphy, Ranking Member DeGette, and Members of the Subcommittee:

Good morning and thank you for this opportunity to provide testimony on the important issue regarding youth and sports-related concussions. I commend you and your colleagues on the work of this committee to shed light on this critical issue. My name is Kelli Jantz, and I am the mom to Jake Snakenburg. My son Jake was your typical all American boy. Devoted to sports, his friends, and our family Jake was often referred to as our "social butterfly". He had a big heart, and genuinely cared for those in his life. He had a joy about him, that others could not resist. His big brother summed it up best when he said "Jake drank up life like it was pouring from a fire hose". He gave 110% in everything, especially sports.

On September 18, 2004 our 14 year old son Jake Snakenburg got up at 6:15AM in anticipation of his football game. Jake loved football and all that it offered, the spirit of competition, the physical challenge and probably most of all the friendships. He was particularly excited about playing in this game as he had been held out of a few practices due to an injury from a prior game. Jake had suffered a hit which left his arms numb and tingly for a few minutes. From what he described we figured he had "tweaked" or strained his neck. He had not lost consciousness, or seen stars, no telltale signs of a major injury. He was monitored the following week and the range of motion in his neck improved. Jake did not inform his father or I of any headaches, but a few friends said Jake had complained of headaches during the week. Regardless, he was able to return to practice and meet the required number of practices to be eligible to play game day.

In warm – ups on the 18th, Jake took a hard hit that appeared to shake him. He noticed me looking on and waved me off to let me know he was ok. As the game began, Jake lined up with his team, but before the snap stumbled forward. The whistle was blown and penalty flag thrown. Slowly Jake got up and headed to the sideline, but collapsed on the field. He did not get up. Jake was unconscious. 911 was called immediately and life flight dispatched to the football field. Jake was airlifted to Swedish Medical. The neurosurgeon advised us that Jake had suffered a head injury and steps were being taken to decrease the swelling in his brain. He told us that Jake may never play his beloved football again, and will have a long recovery. The surgeon followed this statement with "if he survives this injury". Tragically Jake did not survive. It was determined that Jake had suffered what is called Second Impact Syndrome, a condition leading to rapid swelling from more than one concussion, a phenomenon unique to young brains. It is likely Jake suffered a concussion the previous week. The subsequent hits during warm ups, though not associated with a concussion had a compounding effect and continued to further injure his already compromised brain.

Since Jake's death, I have made it my mission to continue to raise awareness of the consequences of concussion in youth sports. Following Jake's death, Karen McAvoy, Psy.D., developed the REAP Project which was adopted by the Rocky Mountain Hospital for Children and is made available to the Colorado Department of Education. The REAP Project is a community-based model for Concussion Management. REAP stands for Remove/Reduce physical and cognitive, or mental demands; Educate the student athlete, families, educators, coaches and medical professionals; Adjust/Accommodate for the student athlete academically; and Pace the student athlete back to learning, activity and play. However, the program addresses all youth with concussions, regardless of cause, meaning not just sports-related concussions, as any concussion can directly impact a student's learning ability. Educators, therefore, should understand the impact of concussions, as well as moderate to severe brain injury, will have with regard to academics.

At least three states have passed legislation to begin addressing academic needs after a concussion, generally referred to as "return to learn", to bring these issues to the attention of educators. And, several states have developed training, resources and consultative teams to assist educators with screening, assessment, educational planning and support for children with brain injury regardless of severity.

I have had the opportunity to support the REAP concussion management program which is now being adopted in other states. The REAP manuals have been funded for free distribution by the Jake Snakenburg Memorial Fund. I have also had the opportunity to testify in hearings leading to the passing of the Jake Snakenburg Youth Concussion Act in 2011, which requires Colorado middle school, junior high and high school coaches, as well as volunteer coaches with regard to recreational sports, to be educated on how to recognize a concussion; to remove players from play, if a concussion is suspected; and to require the student athlete to be signed off by a medical professional before returning to play. All 50 states and the District of Columbia have passed similar legislation.

Looking at the wealth of research on the consequences of youth concussion and the rapidly evolving advances in concussion management, we would be remiss, actually it would be irresponsible, not to take every possible opportunity to develop measures to protect our youth from the devastating disabilities and potential death resulting from these types of injuries. To help determine the extent and resulting problems, the Institute of Medicine and the National Research Council issued a report in October 2013 that called for the Centers for Disease Control and Prevention to establish and oversee a national surveillance system.

Therefore, I support funding in the President's budget ($5 million) to implement the National Concussion Survellience Survey. Without comprehensive data, we will never know how many of our youth have been affected by concussions nor the short-term and long-term consequences. I ask Congress to please include $5 million in the FY2017 budget to allow the CDC to collect data on incidence and prevalence of concussions in youth population. I also support the passage of the Youth Sports Concussion Act, sponsored by the Congressional Brain Injury Task Force Cochairs, Representative Bill Pascrell and Representative Tom Rooney, to ensure that sports equipment is safe.

In addition, I urge the U.S. Department of Education to provide assistance and support to state departments of education and public schools with regard to training educators to better address the academic needs of students with brain injury resulting in cognitive and behavioral problems.

Schools should be encouraged to work with state and local agencies that provide services to individuals with brain injury in order to coordinate community resources and supports to families in order for children who are injured to have a successful recovery and outcome after brain injury. The National Association of State Head Injury Administrators (NASHIA) is one organization which can help identify state resources.

In closing, these children are our future. It is our responsibility as parents, coaches, teacher, medical professionals, policy makers and the community as a whole to make sure we do all we can to support the necessary culture change to make youth sports as safe as possible and protect our children, as well as to provide appropriate treatment and assistance once a concussion occurs.

Thank you for addressing this critical issue and allowing me to participate in the hearing today.

1. Have you ever heard of Second Impact Syndrome? Who is most at risk of getting this?

"NEW SPORTS EXPOSE: CHANGES NEEDED IN ALL DIRECTIONS," BY RALPH NADER, FROM *COMMON DREAMS*, FEBRUARY 26, 2015

Make no mistake about it, sports are important.

That's true if for no other reason than the fact that sports absorb billions of hours of people's time – at all ages. Whatever you think about sports, they're clearly important for that reason alone.

Sports are also important because they have become a multibillion-dollar industry, one of the top ten biggest industries in the country. According to Plunkett Research, the estimated size of the entire sports industry in 2012 was $435 billion. That makes it much bigger than the U.S. auto industry, movie industry and many others.

Sports are important because professional and big-time college sports basically operate as self-regulated monopolies. That creates problems that filter all the way down to sports at the high school and youth levels.

Finally, sports are important because sports ethos, mentalities and policies impact, in one way or another, virtually all aspects of our society.

While sports started as a form of play, recreation, and fun for family and friends, they have increasingly become commercialized and professionalized spectacles, at all levels (See: Little League World Series). The result is our games suffer from a general soul sickness, resulting in problems that are zapping the human spirit out of the games we love at their best.

Clearly, sports are worthy of more serious examination than they receive in the United States today.

Nevertheless, controversial sports problems and abuses haven't received the persistent, timely attention they deserve, including the development of well-conceived remedies for the games' ills.

Until now.

How We Can Save Sports: A Game Plan, by Dr. Ken Reed a former college athlete, coach, long-time sports marketer, sports management instructor and sports issues columnist, and now sports policy director for our

League of Fans (see leagueoffans.org) is unlike any other sports book I've seen.

There are plenty of books on the market about each of our most popular sports – football, basketball, baseball, hockey, tennis, golf, etc. There are numerous books that profile our well-known sports figures. And there are a few books on specific sports issues like concussions and taxpayer-financed stadiums and arenas.

But Reed's book is different. It covers the whole waterfront of sports issues and looks at how they're all interconnected. It's basically a sports manifesto that looks at nine of the most important sports issues we face today and the red thread that weaves through them all, from youth sports to the pros.

And what is that red thread?

According to Reed, it's ego and greed, and the win-at-all-costs (WAAC) and profit-at-all-costs (PAAC) policies and mentalities those vices have spawned throughout the world of sports.

In fact, it is these WAAC and PAAC policies and mentalities that are the foundation of the numerous issues Reed addresses in his book, including: adult-dominated youth sports; the demise of physical education and intramural sports in our schools; militaristic coaches that berate and abuse our young athletes; the lack of adequate concussion safety protocols and return-to-play guidelines throughout sports; a college sports model in which athletes' economic and civil rights are denied; wealthy pro sports owners who hold taxpayers hostage in order to get publicly-financed sports palaces built; and an ongoing lack of equal opportunity in sports for female, disabled, and LGBT athletes and administrators. The list goes on.

One issue that Reed addresses in his book really hits home with me. He points out the fallacy behind the idea that the United States is a "sports mad country" as many outsiders have called us. In effect, we're a country that's mad about spectator sports. Our sports pages should really be renamed "Spectator Sports" because that's all they cover. They have nothing to do with community participatory sports.

Americans love watching sports, usually while sitting on their couches eating junk food. It's interesting to note that in a University of Arkansas, Little Rock study, highly identified sports fans had significantly higher health risk behaviors than non-sports fans on a range of health behavior measures, including a higher Body Mass Index (BMI), along with higher fat, fast food and alcohol consumption.

Reed also takes a jab at the sports media. He points out that the media will occasionally identify scandals, and other symptoms of problems in the sports world, but then stop. What's left missing is a discussion regarding how to mitigate these problems. Also, mostly left out is any reporting of sports reform initiatives and grassroots movements designed to change sport—unless there is a major eruption or scandal that can't be ignored.

Why? Because sports media corporations, and most sports journalists, have too much invested, economically and psychologically in the current system to push for significant change. As Reed says, the dominant ideology of commercialized and professionalized sport is diffused through corporate entities, including sports media.

Therefore, it's up to citizens who love sport at its best, to rise up and push for change. Reed labels his call to action "citizenship through sports activism." He provides would-be sports reformers and activists the analytical foundation, recommendations and resources needed to improve the valuable sports experience for all stakeholders.

He also identifies where people are already fighting for needed change around the country.

That's good news because sports can be healthy socio-cultural practice of much value when win-at-all-cost and profit-at-all-cost thinking aren't driving the bus.

Let's hope that a significant number of sports fans—including concerned parents of young athletes—take Reed's lead and start debating and discussing these issues in their communities.

It's time for a grand slam look at the entire sports scene.

1. According to Ralph Nader, a famous political and environmental activist, how does the sports industry need to be reformed in order to protect athletes?

"TESTIMONY OF ANDREW GREGORY, M.D., BEFORE THE HOUSE SUBCOMMITTEE ON OVERSIGHT AND INVESTIGATION," FROM THE US HOUSE OF REPRESENTATIVES, MAY 13, 2016

Chairman Murphy and Members of the Committee:

My name is Dr. Andrew Gregory. I am a pediatric sports medicine specialist at Vanderbilt University Medical Center. I am a fellow of both the American Academy of Pediatrics and the American College of Sports Medicine as well as a member of USA Football's Medical Advisory Committee. I have served USA Football in this capacity since 2013. I am not a USA Football employee nor do I receive compensation for being on the committee.

USA Football is the sport's national governing body and a member of the U.S. Olympic Committee. We do not operate youth football leagues nor lead high school teams. We create resources and direct programs that establish important standards using the best available science, educating coaches, parents and young athletes who play football.

Our programs are endorsed by more than 40 organizations spanning medicine and sport, including the American College of Sports Medicine, the National Athletic Trainers' Association and the American Medical Society for Sports Medicine.

USA Football is an independent nonprofit organization that works in partnership with the NCAA, NFL, National Federation of State High School Associations and Pop Warner Little Scholars, among others.

The purpose of this testimony is to outline three key elements of how USA Football advances concussion prevention and research for the good of young athletes who play our sport and gain its fitness and social benefits. These three key elements are education, research and innovation.

EDUCATION

USA Football trains more youth and high school football coaches combined than any organization in the United States.

Education has the power to change behavior for the better. This is the core of USA Football's Heads Up Football program, delivered through online courses, in-person clinics and continuing education opportunities.

Its six educational components are:

- CDC-approved concussion recognition and response
- Heat preparedness and hydration
- Sudden cardiac arrest protocols
- Proper equipment fitting
- Tackling techniques
- Blocking techniques

Heads Up Football was introduced nationally to youth football organizations in 2013 and to high schools in 2014. More than 6,300 youth leagues and 1,100 high schools spanning all 50 states and Washington, D.C., representing approximately 1 million players, enrolled in Heads Up Football in 2015.

Coaches enrolled in the program complete hands-on, in-person instruction as well as an online curriculum covering the topics bulleted above. USA Football also trains one representative from each school or youth organization to serve as its Player Safety Coach, reinforcing the program's teachings, guiding practices as needed throughout the season, seeing the skills put into action at games and serving as a resource for players, parents and coaches.

Every youth football coach within an organization enrolled in Heads Up Football is trained how to teach the game's fundamentals by completing USA Football's nationally accredited Level 1 Coaching Certification Course. High school coaches gain training through USA Football's High School Coach Certification course, developed in partnership with the National Federation of State High School Associations.

Heads Up Football is endorsed by 14 state high school associations and 11 state high school coaches associations. The Oregon State Activities Association this year is requiring all football coaches in its 249 football-playing member high schools to participate in Heads Up Football prior to the start of the 2016 season.

Dr. Michael Koester, Chairman of the Oregon School Activities Association Sports Medicine Advisory Committee said:

"The really exciting thing about this program is what happens at the high school level will spread throughout the youth programs in each community. This will allow kids to develop their skills in a culture that shares the same language, same techniques and same safety standards from grade school through high school. ... The committee sees this as a natural next step as we look to innovative ways to minimize the risk of all football injuries, but particularly concussions. This is an opportunity for high school coaches to set a standard for the youth leagues in their communities across the state. Ideally, we'll have youth coaches getting certified as well, allowing for continuity of tackling techniques and safety protocols through an athlete's entire playing experience."

More on USA Football's Heads Up Football program may be found at www.usafootball.com/headsup.

USA Football also has been honored nationally for its work to advance athlete safety by the National Athletic Trainers' Association (NATA), the professional membership association for certified athletic trainers and others who support the athletic training profession. Founded in 1950, the NATA has grown to more than 43,000 members worldwide today. In March of this year, USA Football became the first national governing body of a sport to earn the NATA's Youth Sport Safety Ambassador Award for demonstrating significant contributions to the health and welfare of secondary school student-athletes. NATA's prestigious Youth Sports Safety Award recognizes those who have advanced athlete safety by providing exemplary youth sports safety protocols and advancing the provision of medical care, research, policy change and resource allocation. Along with USA Football, Project ADAM, and U.S. Representative Bill Pascrell, Jr., also were recognized with this honor in March 2016. More details can be found about this award at http://www.nata.org/press-release/031516/natapresents-2016-youth-sports-safety-ambassador-awards-seventh-annual-youth.

Due in part to USA Football's medically endorsed programs and innovations, youth and high school football is changing for the better.

RESEARCH

USA Football advances player safety through supporting independent third-party research.

According to a 2014 Datalys Center for Sports Injury Research and Prevention study, encompassing more than 2,000 youth football players, when compared to leagues that did not employ Heads Up Football, players in leagues that did participate in the program showed:

- 76 percent reduction in all injuries during practices
- 38 percent reduction in all injuries during games
- 34 percent decline in concussions during practices
- 29 percent decline in concussions during games

The peer-reviewed study was published by The Orthopaedic Journal of Sports Medicine in July 2015.

A subset of this study encompassing 70 youth players showed that over the course of a season, those in leagues enrolled in Heads Up Football had 2-to-3 less head impacts of 10g or greater per practice compared to those in non-Heads Up Football leagues. This may prevent more than 100 such impacts over the course of a 12-week season.

"This is compelling data," Datalys Center President and Injury Epidemiologist Dr. Thomas Dompier said. "I am actually surprised by the strength of the association but completely confident in our findings. It's logical – in the first two years of research, we found that coach and player behavior was predictive of injury even though we hypothesized differently. That led us to pursue a third year of research to examine if coach education reduced injuries and head impacts, and we found that this was the case."

Dompier continued: "If we had found that only injury rates or only head impacts were reduced but not both, I would not have been as confident with our results. However, combined with the first two years of data that pointed at coach and player behavior, these current data indicate that coach education can have a positive impact on player safety and may serve as a model for youth sports like soccer, ice hockey, lacrosse and others concerned with concussion and head impact risk."

On the high school level, Fairfax County Public Schools, the 10th largest school district in the country, has employed Heads Up Football since 2013. In this time, the district has reported a 43.3 percent decline in concussions among its 3,000 football-playing student athletes.

During this same time span with all 25 of its high school programs enrolled in Heads Up Football, overall football injuries have declines 23.9 percent. Data was collected by Fairfax County Public Schools' athletic trainers. "We have one consistent match of what we're talking about, of how we're teaching our athletes to play the game. From ankle biter through 12th grade, we have one consistent curriculum," said Bill Curran, Director of Student Activities and Athletics for Fairfax County School District. "We're able to show with data that there's a difference. You know, Centreville High School played in back-to-back state championships and had the fewest injuries of our 25 high schools. That's a big deal."

Similarly, high schools within the South Bend (Ind.) Community School Corporation (SBCSC), with approximately 1,000 football-playing student-athletes, reported concussions from football to decline by 40 percent from 2014 to 2015, the first year the school system implemented Heads Up Football district-wide. Although football participation increased across the district from 1,000 student-athletes to 1,037 during this time, concussions from football decreased from 53 to 32. Concussion data was recorded by the high schools' athletic trainers. "USA Football's 'Heads Up Football' program has been invaluable to us and we are so happy to have had the opportunity to become a part of the program," SBCSC Athletic Director Kirby Whitacre said.

USA Football is committed to continue commissioning independent studies into youth and high school player health and safety.

INNOVATION

USA Football provides practice guidelines, practice planning tools and defined Levels of Contact (www.usa-football.com/health-safety/levels-of-contact) for tackle coaches to properly teach player techniques in a progressive manner. More young football players than ever before are learning the fundamentals in a gradual and appropriate manner prior to advancing to full contact. Endorsed by the American College of Sports Medicine, the American Medical Society for Sports Medicine and the National Athletic Trainers' Association, USA Football's Youth Practice Guidelines set important standards for preseason heat acclimatization, regulating practice intensity and maintaining hydration levels to reduce the risk of injury and create the best environment for our children.

Among its pillars:

- No two-a-day practices in preseason or regular season
- Graduated equipment and contact levels in preseason to properly acclimate players to exercise and heat
- No more than two hours of practice in any day
- No more than four football activity days per week, including practices and games
- No more than 30 minutes of Live Action or "Thud" level contact per day
- USA Football's Levels of Contact focus on varying intensity levels throughout practices to build player confidence, ensure their safety and prevent both physical and mental exhaustion. Five intensity levels are used to introduce players to practice drills which position them to master the fundamentals and increase skill development.
- Air – Players run a drill unopposed and without contact
- Bags – Drill is run against a bag or other soft-contact surface
- Control – Drill is run at assigned speed with predetermined winner. Contact remains above the waist and players stay on their feet.

- Thud – Drill is run at competitive speed with no predetermined winner. Players stay on their feet and a quick whistle ends the drill. It is important to note that USA Football considers "Thud" to be a full-contact level and limits the time that coaches can run drills at this speed and intensity. Other organizations – including the Ivy League and other college programs – do not include "Thud" as full contact.
- Live action – Game-like conditions and the only time players are taken to the ground.

Through innovations such as the Youth Practice Guidelines and Levels of Contact, coaches instruct their players through a series of USA Football-developed drills to build confidence and instill the proper fundamentals. Through a player progression development model, players learn the right stage at the right age, using the same terminology as they mature mentally, physical and emotionally.

USA Football's Heads Up Tackling technique teaches young athletes to make contact with their shoulders in an ascending strike and rip their arms up through the ball-carrier, grabbing the backside of the jersey – thus keeping the head and eyes up through the process. Likewise, USA Football's Heads Up Blocking technique takes a player from stance to steps to contact, using their hands – not their helmets – to drive opponents out of the way. Laying the basic foundations, Heads Up Tackling and Heads Up Blocking fundamentals can be used to teach every type of tackle and block that a player needs to learn.

As Dr. Jon Devine, president of the American Medical Society for Sports Medicine, said: "We endorsed USA Football's Heads Up Football program in 2014, and it continues to advance player safety and change behavior for the better. Young athletes are safer when their coaches are trained, proper fundamentals are taught and protocols in the best available science are put into motion. Creating a program like Heads Up Football takes leadership – leadership one would expect from a national governing body of sport."

USA Football works every day to improve education, establish research and pave innovation toward creating a better, safer game for the young athletes who enjoy the fun, exercise and social benefits of an exceptional team sport.

1. What do you think about these youth practice guidelines? If you play football, do you follow such guidelines with your team?

"N.F.L.-BACKED YOUTH PROGRAM SAYS IT REDUCED CONCUSSIONS. THE DATA DISAGREES," BY ALAN SCHWARZ, FROM THE *NEW YORK TIMES*, JULY 27, 2016

As increasing numbers of parents keep their children from playing tackle football for safety reasons, the National

Football League and other groups have sought to reassure them that the game is becoming less dangerous.

No initiative has received more backing and attention than Heads Up Football, a series of in-person and online courses for coaches to learn better safety procedures and proper tackling drills. The N.F.L. funds and heavily promotes the program. The league and U.S.A. Football, youth football's governing body, which oversees the program, have sold Heads Up Football to thousands of leagues and parents as having been proved effective — telling them that an independent study showed the program reducing injuries by 76 percent and concussions by about 30 percent.

That study, published in July 2015, showed no such thing, a review by The New York Times has found. The research and interviews with people involved with it indicate, rather, that Heads Up Football showed no demonstrable effect on concussions during the study, and significantly less effect on injuries over all, than U.S.A. Football and the league have claimed in settings ranging from online materials to congressional testimony.

As the 2016 youth football season dawns, the revelation will most likely fuel skeptics of football's claims of reform, and discourage parents who want solid information about the sport's risks for their children.

"Everybody who is involved in trying to improve the safety of youth sports, when parents such as myself are so desperate to have effective solutions, has the responsibility to make sure that any information that they are putting out to the public is accurate, is comprehensive, and is based on legitimate science," said Elliot F. Kaye, the chairman of the United States Consumer Product Safety Commission, who has worked with U.S.A. Football and the N.F.L. on improving helmet safety. "It does not appear that this met that standard."

Representatives of U.S.A. Football and the N.F.L. said in interviews that they had been unaware that their claims of Heads Up Football's effectiveness were unsupported by the study, which was conducted by the Datalys Center for Sports Injury Research and Prevention through a $70,000 grant from U.S.A. Football.

"U.S.A. Football erred in not conducting a more thorough review with Datalys to ensure that our data was up to date," Scott Hallenbeck, the executive director of U.S.A. Football, said in an email to The Times. "We regret that error." He added that the material would be removed from the organization's print and online materials, and that "our partners and constituents" would be notified of the errors.

Brian McCarthy, an N.F.L. spokesman, said that the league would also include updated information from now on.

Both U.S.A. Football and the league said that the questionable data and conclusions were actually preliminary results provided by Datalys five months before the study was published. The lead researchers for Datalys, Thomas Dompier and Zachary Kerr, confirmed in interviews that, despite knowing that the final paper contradicted their preliminary claims, they did not inform U.S.A. Football of this until last month, one day after speaking with The Times.

Mr. Dompier, the president of Datalys, said in an interview: "We're the ones that put out the numbers. We're the ones that kind of blew it."

In an email, Mr. Kerr said that the company had released the early data because, "The results were so compelling, we felt morally obligated to make the youth football community aware of the results."

CONFLICTING DATA

The N.F.L. and its players' union formed U.S.A. Football in 2002 to oversee the sport and help it grow among children ages 6 to 14. But participation has dropped precipitously in recent years, from 3 millionin 2010 to about 2.2 million last fall — a decline generally attributed to concerns about injuries, particularly to the brain.

In 2013, in consultation with the N.F.L., U.S.A. Football started Heads Up Football, whose primary goals were to improve safety and reassure parents. The program requires one "player safety coach" per team to attend a clinic that focuses on concussion recognition and response, blocking and tackling techniques, proper hydration and other safety topics. A team's other coaches must take online courses in those subjects as well.

In March 2014, the N.F.L. gave U.S.A. Football $45 million, in large part to get more youth leagues to adopt the program.

While U.S.A. Football is said to operate independently from the N.F.L., the league is its primary source of operating funds, and some researchers consider the two almost indistinguishable.

"In my mind, U.S.A. Football and the N.F.L. are one," said Dawn Comstock, a professor of epidemiology and the primary researcher into high school sports injuries at the Colorado School of Public Health. "If I'm talking with one about something involving youth football safety, my perception is I'm talking to both."

Dr. Comstock said that in July 2014, Jeff Miller, the N.F.L.'s senior vice president for health and safety policy, and David Krichavsky, then its director of player health and safety, asked her to propose some studies that would, she said, "highlight the potential positive aspects" of youth football's safety initiatives and provide "a potential positive take-home message for parents." Dr. Comstock said that she had provided some ideas but that the league did not pursue.

Mr. McCarthy, of the N.F.L., said in an email on Monday, "Our only interest is in research that will help us determine the efficacy of these and other programs and how we can make the game safer."

Also in 2014, U.S.A. Football asked Datalys, an Indianapolis-based firm that handles all of the N.C.A.A.'s injury research, to monitor injury rates during that fall season among six youth leagues that used Heads Up Football and four leagues that did not, covering more than 2,000 players.

In February 2015, Datalys gave U.S.A. Football the results: Leagues that used Heads Up Football had 76 percent fewer injuries, 34 percent fewer concussions in games and 29 percent fewer concussions in practices.

In U.S.A. Football's blog post announcing that the safety program "reduces injuries," Mr. Dompier said: "This is compelling data. I am actually surprised by the strength of the association but completely confident in our findings."

These figures were prominently reported in the news media and on websites of youth leagues as a means to show parents that Heads Up Football was scientifically sound. N.F.L. promotional materials have called the program "The New Standard in Football;" a page in its 2015 Information Guide is headlined, "Study Finds U.S.A. Football Program Advances Player Safety."

But last summer, when The Orthopaedic Journal of Sports Medicine published Datalys's formal paper on the study, the paper did not include the same injury and concussion figures. Its data actually told a far different story about Heads Up Football's effectiveness.

Rather than looking at Heads Up Football leagues in one category, the paper instead split them into two groups: those that did or did not also belong to Pop Warner Football, a division of youth leagues that has added its own rules to mitigate injuries. Pop Warner leagues have disallowed certain head-on blocking and tackling drills and drastically reduced full-contact practice time, measures that were not a part of U.S.A. Football's program.

As it turned out, only leagues that adhered to Pop Warner's rules saw a meaningful drop in concussions. Leagues that used Heads Up Football alone actually saw slightly higher concussion rates, although that uptick was not statistically significant. The previously reported drops were clearly driven by a league's affiliation with Pop Warner, not Heads Up Football.

Similarly, Heads Up Football leagues saw no change in injuries sustained during games unless they also used Pop Warner's practice restrictions. The drop in practice injuries among Heads Up Football-only leagues was 63 percent, but combined with in-game injuries, the total reduction became about 45 percent — far less than the

76 percent presented by U.S.A. Football and the N.F.L. for the past year and a half.

The authors did not address how the paper's data contradicted their preliminary conclusions from five months before. Regarding the fact that Datalys did not inform U.S.A. Football or the N.F.L. of the discrepancies, Mr. Kerr said in an email: "Datalys stands by our decision to release preliminary data in our Feb 2015 release because if we prevented even one youth football player from suffering an injury (sprain, fracture, strain, severe contusion, or concussion), then the release was a success."

There are other instances when Datalys has presented data to the public that differed from its scientific papers.

A "Youth Football Fact Sheet" for the public on the Datalys website lists the most common injuries sustained by youngsters, as determined by a separate study it conducted for U.S.A. Football three years ago. But it has significant differences from the list in a paper the company published last year, also in The Orthopaedic Journal of Sports Medicine. For example, the paper's listing for "Nervous System (stinger)," which comprised 4.2 percent of injuries, does not appear on the fact sheet; that slot is filled instead by "Wind Knocked Out" (4.1 percent), a category that does not appear in the paper.

Mr. Dompier said in an email that the category for stinger — where a blow to the spine causes extreme pain and numbness through the arms — was renamed Wind Knocked Out because both are neurological injuries, and the latter would be more recognized by parents.

CREDIT, WITH A CAVEAT

A spokesman for U.S.A. Football, Steve Alic, said that research conducted outside Datalys has shown the effectiveness of Heads Up Football. He cited the Fairfax County public school system in Virginia, which has seen a 24 percent decrease in total injuries and a 43 percent drop in concussions since adopting the program in 2013.

Bill Curran, the county's director of student activities and athletics, confirmed those numbers and praised Heads Up Football's safety initiatives for contributing to them. He added that Fairfax County went well beyond the Heads Up program, though, in ways that included drastically reducing full-contact practice time during the season to 90 minutes per week, whereas before, he said, "we probably had some teams doing 90 minutes in a single practice."

"I give them a huge amount of credit," Mr. Curran said of U.S.A. Football's efforts. "But it takes a hell of a lot more than going to their website and taking the online courses and getting accreditation."

As the 2016 season approaches, the faulty pronouncements about the research continue to be cited by youth programs and football officials as evidence that Heads Up Football makes football safer, especially regarding concussions. During a high school sports conference in Alabama last week, a coach presented a glowing slide show about the program to fellow coaches and athletic directors, unaware that many of the numbers and statements were not supported by the data.

Last May, coaches from Columbia High School in Maplewood, N.J., invited some eighth-graders interested in playing football to a meeting in the cafeteria.

"They basically said they teach Heads Up Football, which reduced head injuries and concussions," said Jacob Kasdan, one of the students who attended the meeting. "I think they're struggling to find enough players."

Jacob went home and asked if he could play this fall. His father declined to sign the forms.

1. What change to youth football practices contributed to the most statistically significant decrease in injuries?

CHAPTER 5

WHAT THE MEDIA SAY

This chapter raises the age-old question as to what should the media's role be. Is it the media's job to simply present the facts or to take a particular stand and advocate for change? Is it irresponsible to criticize the current system without offering solutions?

Many have—fairly or unfairly—criticized the media for both overemphasizing the dangers of contact sports for young people and underemphasizing it. It is a passionate issue, and advocates on both sides want the media to support their positions.

There can also be a divide—maybe based in age—on how the issue is covered. There was never talk of concussions or head injuries twenty-five years ago, and it is true that many former professional football players never suffered lingering effects at all. But now the issue is widely discussed, and the younger generation of reporters are clearly advocating for change and improved safety.

Early on, the reporting also centered mainly on injuries suffered by professional athletes, while now the emphasis has shifted to those playing and coaching youth sports.

"FROM CHEERLEADING TO MMA, CHANCE FOR CONCUSSION IS HARD TO ELIMINATE," BY BLANE FERGUSON, FROM *CRONKITE NEWS*, APRIL 28, 2015

At first glance, mixed martial arts and cheerleading appear to be at the opposite ends of the safety spectrum. But they share similar concerns and protocols when it comes to concussions.

Bottom line: Beware. At the youth level, both can be hazardous to your health.

Ankle injuries, hand injuries and muscle injuries are common in cheerleading, said Jennifer Lannon, owner of the Arizona All-Stars cheerleading program. But so are concussions.

"If something does happen and they do get a concussion or they do have a head injury, we don't move them," Lannon said. "Typically, what our protocol is we assess the situation and then from there, we will call 911 if needed."

With situations involving stunt maneuvers and potentially dangerous outcomes only a slight mistake away, cheerleading, like other sports, is prone to head collisions.

At a competition in Palm Springs, California, 15-year-old cheerleader Madison Woolgar warmed up with her team outside the hotel in a grassy area.

"We do a stunt where we throw the flier and she stands on another girl and then comes down toward us," Woolgar said. "It went crooked and she landed on my head, her elbow and knee went into my head and then I passed out and it went from there."

Karlee Brown, 12, says she suffered a concussion but only sat out a day before returning to practice for a weekend competition.

"I tried practicing on Friday, I had a headache, and then I was just kind of a little dizzy at the end but I just had to push through it."

Accidents like this are common in cheerleading. Lannon recalls a recent injury occurring in practice involving a young girl who hit her head.

"She was on the bottom of a pyramid and the pyramid came down," Lannon said. "The knee went into her head and she was fine when she got down and then she progressively got worse."

Lannon then called 911.

Then there's mixed martial arts, a sport in which contact is the name of the game.

"Smiling" Sam Alvey is a professional fighter competing in the Ultimate Fighting Championship promotion. He is also the head MMA instructor for children at Dan Henderson's Athletic Fitness Center in Temecula, California.

According to the United States Fight League, head strikes are prohibited for fighters under the age of 16.

"They (the parents) don't want their kids getting punched," Alvey said. "I say, 'That's not what we're teaching them. Maybe in 10 years we can start working on some headshots, but right now they're just kids.' I'm not a neurosurgeon, but I know getting hit in the head is bad for you, especially at such a young age."

Still, incidental head contact occurs.

"I tell the kid who made the contact why it was wrong and what happened," Alvey said. "Nobody is doing it on purpose, but accidents do happen."

It wasn't always like this. Before concussions and head trauma came under the microscope, practices at many levels of MMA, especially at the professional level, featured hard, often grueling sparring. Now, training is focused on sparring correctly rather than brutally.

"You don't need to take sparring out," said Chael Sonnen, ESPN analyst and former UFC fighter. "You just need to be a good partner and then you have to work out with a guy who is a good partner."

Former UFC fighter Aaron Simpson, one of the owners of Power MMA and Fitness in Gilbert, said technique is getting better.

"We don't just send a guy in and spar five times a week and they get a brain injury the next day and come back to training and spar again," Simpson. "I mean, if you get knocked out you're out for a while. It takes a long time and we understand this now, it takes a long time for your brain to heal."

In a sport where one of the main objectives at the professional level is to knock your opponent out, it would be nearly impossible to eliminate concussions altogether.

Dr. Ken Ota, a ringside physician with the Arizona Boxing and MMA Commission, believes the sport should discuss how to avoid concussions in MMA. But there's a more realistic approach.

"At this point that would be to figure out how is it that we screen fighters initially trying to obtain data," Ota said. "Telling us what their baseline cognitive status, neurological status, neuropsychological status is so that we can measure it over time to determine a threshold at which we should probably be advising them, 'Look it may be time to retire from the sport.'"

Regardless of the sport, there's an inherent risk for injury – and it's not just limited to cheerleading or MMA.

"I don't understand why a person would want to jump out of an airplane," Sonnen said. "I can't wrap my head around that, but I damn sure want them to have that choice."

1. What do you think about Chael Sonnen's last quote in this article about allowing young people the right to choose to participate in high-risk sports? Do you agree or disagree?

"PRO FOOTBALL'S UNSPORTSMANLIKE CONDUCT," BY BILL MOYERS, FROM *COMMON DREAMS*, SEPTEMBER 17, 2013

When Thomas Jefferson wrote that all men are created equal, his Monticello farm team was obviously not what he had in mind. They were chattel, possessions toiling in his fields. So it's not lightly — or unreasonable — to invoke the plantation mentality to describe the National Football League.

Tom Van Riper, who covers sports for *Forbes* magazine, points out that of the 31 owners of NFL teams, seventeen — more than half — are billionaires. Many boast of being self-made, in the image of Horatio Alger, but are now ensconced in luxury skyboxes far above the proletarians whose own dreams of glory ride vicariously on the grunts and groans of bulky but agile gladiators only one play away from a career-ending collision with the laws of physics.

For more than a year, public television's award-winning investigative journalism series *FRONTLINE* had been collaborating on a new documentary about brain trauma in pro football with journalists from ESPN, the giant sports network. The title: "League of Denial: The NFL's Concussion Crisis."

A hard-hitting promo for the investigation upset ESPN President John Skipper. "Over the top" was his description — too "sensational." He was so "startled" — his word — that he pulled the plug on ESPN's partnership with *FRONTLINE*. The network has had a reputation for solid, even bold reporting of controversy and scandal in pro and amateur athletics. Not this time.

You have to ask, what was the actual reason for ESPN's decision? Could it really be what John Skipper claims? Or is it that NFL games are, as *The New York Times* recently wrote, "probably the most valuable commodity in televised sports." ESPN is paying $15.2 billion — billion! — for the rights to telecast "Monday Night Football" for 10 years through the year 2021, but it then reaps a fortune in advertising and subscriber fees. The monthly price to watch ESPN is four times higher than the next most expensive national cable network. More than $6 billion are hauled in from cable every year. It's the cash cow for the entire Disney empire. In an interview with the *Times*, former Disney CEO Michael Eisner said, "To this day, the Walt Disney Company would not exist without ESPN. The protection of Mickey Mouse is ESPN."

Shortly before his decision, John Skipper had lunch with NFL Commissioner Roger Goodell and two others in New York City. Sources told the *Times*, "The meeting was combative... with league officials conveying their irritation with the direction of the documentary." Skipper also admitted to ESPN's independent ombudsman Robert Lipsyte that he had spoken with Disney chairman and CEO Bob Iger. But he insists that the choice to remove ESPN from the *FRONTLINE* investigation was his own.

Whether coincidence or not, just after ESPN's decision to disassociate itself from *FRONTLINE*, the NFL settled a class-action suit brought by thousands of retired players and their families seeking damages from injuries linked to concussions. To the casual fan, it was a win for the players — a sum of $765 million. But even if they finally have to cough up, the owners will feel no pain. That's just a fraction of the estimated $10 billion the league generates in revenue every year. The typical payout per plaintiff will amount to around $150,000 — not nearly enough to cover a lifetime of lost wages and medical bills faced by the victims of serious brain trauma.

These players and their families haven't won much. It isn't even a tie. "Pitiless" was the description of the settlement by *The Nation* magazine's sportswriter Dave Zirin. And as another formidable sleuth of journalism, David Cay Johnston, recently asked in the *Columbia Journalism Review*, "If the settlement does not cover all the costs of medical care, much less lost future wages, who will bear that burden?"

His answer: taxpayers.

When players are no longer insured by the league and find themselves unable to afford private insurance for their enduring afflictions, taxpayers — all of us — will be the ones to pay, through Medicaid and Social Security disability.

We won't even be allowed to see the NFL's own extensive research into the neurological damage caused by concussions; the settlement allows the League and the owners to keep it under lock and key.

Football, like politics, "ain't beanbag." The fortunes of players can vanish in a single blow, while high in their plush digs, owners reap continuing gains from TV and advertising and the tax breaks and subsidies showered on them by compliant politicians. Big-time sports mirror the vast inequality that has come to define America in this century.

Something else to remember as we relax in our favorite easy chair, dazzled and thrilled by men who can be hurt for life. If their world were just, they would not be so matter-of-factly tossed aside, we might think twice about how we want to be entertained, and the owners of capital would be amply penalized for unsportsmanlike conduct.

Fortunately, we can still see "League of Denial" on *FRONTLINE* beginning October 8. Unfortunately, the title won't be just a metaphor.

1. In this article, Bill Moyers is highly critical of the NFL and their policies involving football injuries. Do you think football fans can, morally speaking, watch their sport knowing the dangers these players face?

"CONCUSSIONS AREN'T ONLY A MEDICAL ISSUE," BY MATT VENTRESCA, FROM *THE CONVERSATION*, JULY 16, 2015

The sports media has a fascination with concussions. Not only is there a huge volume of stories about the issue, but there's also an urgency to the tone of the reporting. The heightened coverage has served to increase awareness of the concussion problem and encourage public debate about sport, health and safety.

But what's often missing from the media's discussion of the topic is a recognition that the concussion problem is not merely a health issue: it's also a *social issue.* We're generally less inclined to look at how concerns about head injuries influence our understanding of ourselves and the identities of others.

Sport plays a significant role in our culture. It's used as a lens to discuss what it means to be a man or woman, how to belong to a nation or community, or how hard work can overcome long odds.

Shouldn't our conversations about a topic that could change the very nature of sport also consider these social and cultural issues?

The absence of social commentary stems from a tendency in the mainstream media to frame concussions as a science and technology problem. Scientists have undertaken essential research that has helped us learn about what happens to the brain after a concussion. Meanwhile, groundbreaking investigative reports and documentaries have made the results of this research accessible to the general population to the point where the symptoms of Chronic Traumatic Encephalopathy have become part of everyday dialogue about sport.

The media is also keen to cover the latest technological breakthrough for new "concussion-resistant" helmets, but just as quick to report on rulings requiring companies to withdraw claims about the superior protection offered by their products. The bulk of the coverage of concussions in the media seems to be organized around one basic understanding: to solve the "concussion crisis" and make sports safer, *we simply need better science.*

I certainly don't want to downplay the scientific advances made by concussion researchers or claim to know more about the brain than neuroscientists. But as the media places so much emphasis on the science behind the concussion debates, important cultural factors are left largely untouched.

One of these factors involves how we make sense of the concussion problem within the hyper-masculine culture of many sports. Most commentators will concede that the era of shaking off a head injury as "getting your bell rung" is over. But the concussion issue should force us to re-think the value systems that make violence and playing through pain manly symbols of toughness.

Ideas about gender even influence how we define the scope of the concussion problem. There are important gender differences, for example, in how often athletes report head injuries, with women tending to report at significantly higher rates than men. Some analysts have pointed to how men could be more likely to "play through" a concussion to live up to masculine ideals of toughness. These same stereotypes might also lead coaches and trainers to be more attuned to the head injuries of female athletes.

In addition to gender, socioeconomic status may influence reporting rates – as well as which athletes choose to play violent sports. When NFL defensive back Richard Sherman spoke out about changes to the NFL's concussion protocol last season, he made strong statements about the role that socioeconomic status plays in how people would react to the concussion problem. Sherman wrote, "People are always going to play football, and if higher income families choose to pull their kids out of the sport, it will only broaden the talent pool, giving underprivileged kids more opportunities to make college rosters."

Similarly, safety Brandon Meriweather made waves later that season by claiming that the league's new concussion rules force defensive players to hit opponents low rather than head on. Meriweather went on to say that the new rules meant he would have no choice but to hit players in the knees, "tear people's ACLs" and "end people's careers" (he's assuming, apparently, that a concussion is less likely to end a player's career than a torn knee ligament).

You don't have to agree with Sherman or Meriweather to recognize that the concussion issue relates to people's work and careers, and athletes from a lower socioeconomic class might think they have more at stake than someone with a more privileged upbringing. Beyond the medical ramifications of concussions, it's important to look at how being diagnosed with a concussion might (or might not) be perceived as affecting an athlete's career or financial goals. This applies to professional athletes, but also rings true for aspiring professional athletes or those with athletic scholarships. Even at the youth or recreational levels, how concussions are diagnosed and treated can be influenced by an athlete's access to health care or his or her ability to take time off from work or school.

Social determinants of health – the social and economic factors that impact health for different groups of people – need to become a bigger part of the way we talk about concussions. Yes, policy and rule changes are important, but so is looking at how the media packages this issue for consumers.

This involves admitting that there might be limits to what folks in white coats can tell us from looking at brain scans or tissue slides. The conversation needs to shift from the comfortable confines of the lab and into the messy world of identity and politics. Only then will the thousands of athletes, coaches, and parents affected by concussions have a clearer picture of how complex the solutions to this problem might actually be.

> 1. How might gender and socioeconomic status change how people report or think about brain injuries in sports?

"A NEW WAY TO CARE FOR YOUNG BRAINS," BY BILL PENNINGTON, FROM THE *NEW YORK TIMES*, MAY 5, 2013

BOSTON — The drumbeat of alarming stories linking concussions among football players and other athletes to brain disease has led to a new and mushrooming American phenomenon: the specialized youth sports concussion clinic, which one day may be as common as a mall at the edge of town.

In the last three years, dozens of youth concussion clinics have opened in nearly 35 states — outpatient centers often connected to large hospitals that are now filled with young athletes complaining of headaches, amnesia, dizziness or problems concentrating. The proliferation of clinics, however, comes at a time when there is still no agreed-upon, established formula for treating the injuries.

"It is inexact, a science in its infancy," said Dr. Michael O'Brien of the sports concussion clinic at Boston Children's Hospital. "We know much more than we once did, but there are lots of layers we still need to figure out."

Deep concern among parents about the effects of concussions is colliding with the imprecise understanding of the injury. To families whose anxiety has been stoked by reports of former N.F.L. players with degenerative brain disease, the new facilities are seen as the most expert care available. That has parents parading to the clinic waiting rooms.

The trend is playing out vividly in Boston, where the phone hardly stops ringing at the youth sports concussion clinic at Massachusetts General Hospital.

"Parents call saying, 'I saw a scary report about concussions on Oprah or on the 'Doctors' show or Katie Couric's show,'" Dr. Barbara Semakula said, describing a typical day at the clinic. "Their child just hurt his head, and they've already leapt to the worst possible scenarios. It's a little bit of a frenzy out there."

About three miles away, at Boston Children's Hospital, patient visits per month to its sports concussion clinic have increased more than fifteenfold in the last five years, to 400 from 25. The clinic, which once consisted of two consultation rooms, now employs nine doctors at four locations and operates six days a week.

"It used to be a completely different scene, with a child's father walking in reluctantly to tell us, 'He's fine; this concussion stuff is nonsense,' " said Dr. William Meehan, a clinic co-founder. "It's totally the opposite now. A kid has one concussion, and the parents are very worried about how he'll be functioning at 50 years old."

Doctors nationwide say the new focus on the dangers of concussions is long overdue. Concerned parents are properly seeking better care, which has saved and improved lives. But a confluence of outside forces has also spawned a mania of sorts that has turned the once-ignored concussion into the paramount medical fear of young athletes across the country.

Most prominent have been news media reports about scores of relatively young former professional athletes reporting serious cognitive problems and other later-life illnesses. Several ex-N.F.L. players who have committed suicide, most notably Junior Seau, a former San Diego Chargers and New England Patriots star, have been found posthumously to have had a degenerative brain disease linked to repeated head trauma.

State legislatures have commanded the attention of families as well, with 43 states passing laws requiring school-age athletes who have sustained a concussion to have written authorization from a medical professional, often one trained in concussion management, before they can return to their sport.

The two Boston clinics, one started in 2007 and the other in 2011, are typical examples of the concussion clinic phenomenon, busy centers of a new branch of American health care and windows into the crux of a mounting youth sports fixation.

"We are really in the trenches of a new medical experience," said Richard Ginsburg, the director of psychological services at Massachusetts General Hospital's youth sports concussion clinic. "First of all, there's some hysteria, so a big part of our job is to educate people that 90 percent of concussions are resolved in a month, if not sooner. As for the other 10 percent of patients, they need somewhere to go.

"So we see them. We see it all."

UNCERTAINTY AMONG DOCTORS

Dr. Rebekah Mannix, an emergency room physician and a concussion researcher at Boston Children's Hospital, works at the front lines of the new world of youth concussion management. Mannix had a concussion while playing college rugby in 1989. After visiting a nearby hospital emergency room, she recalled, she received little guidance about what to expect next — and there was no specialized center to visit if typical concussion symptoms like a headache, nausea, amnesia, fogginess or dizziness persisted.

"They took care of me, but there wasn't much to say because there wasn't a lot known," Mannix said.

Nearly 25 years later, much is still unknown about the roughly four million concussions diagnosed annually in America (millions more probably go undiagnosed). And even with the increased attention to the injury, modern concussion treatment has become a mix of practices derived from prevailing wisdom and experience, limited clinical science and common sense.

"Head injury in general is a strangely archaic field," Mannix said. "There is no predictability. I cannot say to patient A, 'You are going to be fine in a week.' I cannot say to a patient B, 'You are going to be really sick for three months.' "

There is no test or procedure, for example, to verify whether a patient has had a concussion. It is a diagnosis based on a doctor's examination, observation of symptoms and understanding of the incident that led to the injury.

Brain scans can look for bleeding, but they do not identify a concussion, and they come with risks.

"We're very afraid these days of radiology to pediatric brains," Mannix said. "There are times when a scan is the right thing to do, but in the considerable majority of cases, it is not."

Talking parents out of unnecessary brain scans and repeatedly informing them that a high percentage of concussions will not cause lingering symptoms may be the best medicine given by concussion doctors. They say it is the best way to assuage the panic they hear in the voices of parents and patients.

"We get the Junior Seau question a lot. 'Is that what my kid is going to be like?' " O'Brien, of the Boston Children's clinic, said. "Parents are sitting in our office wringing their hands with nervousness."

Paul McDonough of Quincy, Mass., whose daughter, Erin, is a high school hockey player and cheerleader who has had three concussions, said: "When you're reading autopsy results of N.F.L. players with head trauma, as a parent, it doesn't make you very patient or put you at ease. That's why we're all going to specialists."

Erin McDonough saw Dr. Cynthia Stein at the Boston Children's clinic. Among the things Stein routinely explains to patients is that pro football players like Seau may have taken thousands of hits to the head in youth leagues, high school and college — in addition to 10 or more years in the N.F.L.

"Who knows how many concussions someone like Junior Seau really had?" Stein said. "And we don't know why he died. It's not an appropriate comparison. Our patients, if their concussions are managed properly, are going to heal on their own. The body knows how to take care of itself."

But complicating the care is the belief that the recovery time for younger concussion patients will be longer.

"A concussion might be the only injury where the younger you are, the longer it takes to get better," Stein said. "Anything else, if you cut your hand or whatever, the younger you are, the quicker you heal. But for a concussion, recent studies indicate that a 10-year-old heals slower than a 14-year-old, and a 14-year-old heals slower than a 17-year-old."

But there is no wall chart or medical textbook that says just how much rest or inactivity a 10-year-old concussion patient needs to recover compared with a 14-year-old. Every case, regardless of age, can be different based on a multitude of factors, from the severity of the original head injury to genetic, biomedical or anatomical characteristics. Other weighty considerations include the number of previous concussions sustained by a patient and when those concussions occurred.

The lack of guidelines frustrates athletes and their parents, and can confound doctors. In this setting, determining when a young athlete is ready to return to a contact sport, or to school for the mental rigor of regular class work, becomes a highly nuanced, open-ended calculation.

"Parents will get irritated and say, 'It's three weeks and he still has headaches — the last concussion he had, he was better in a day,' " Stein said. "They want a fix. The changing timetables can be trying. But I tell them that you can't try harder to heal the brain, just like you can't try harder to make a broken leg heal faster."

Stein added: "No one would ask someone wearing a cast on their leg to run 10 miles, because we all know that's dangerous. Just because you can't see a concussion like you can see a cast, that doesn't make it any less dangerous if you don't rest it."

RISK OF REPEAT INJURIES

In keeping with its scientifically indefinite nature, concussion management has few collectively recognized, widely acknowledged tenets. But if there is one that is accepted with only a modicum of enduring debate, it is the understanding that athletes who have had a concussion go through a period shortly after the injury during which they are especially vulnerable to catastrophic injury if subjected to another blow to the head. In the worst case, known as second-impact syndrome, it can be a fatal combination.

The chief goal of youth concussion clinics, and the chief purpose of the widespread concussion-related state legislation, is to protect those susceptible to repeat concussions in this period of vulnerability. But no one knows just how long or short that period is.

One of the most commonly known treatment protocols is cognitive rest, which often means avoiding mental stimulation like video games, television or situations with bright lights or loud noises for an extended period after the injury. It is sometimes referred to as the "two weeks lying in a cool, dark room" therapy. Like so many things in concussion management, it has been supported by anecdotal case studies but is unverified by standardized clinical trials.

Dr. Walter Panis, a neurologist at the Massachusetts General clinic, said: "Two weeks in a cool, dark room? Good for mushrooms, bad for people."

At the clinics in Boston and at others nationwide, determining how much activity and stimulation are appropriate, and how soon to introduce them after a concussion, is now done on a case-by-case basis. There is evidence that certain step-by-step treatment schedules have been successful, but therapies considered standard two years ago — like two weeks in a cool, dark room — are being challenged.

"When you get a concussion, you're probably feeling lousy, so you do need some rest," Panis said. "You do need to avoid being stimulated by everything because it will make you feel worse. But that shouldn't last for too long."

Although less controversial, another misunderstood tool in the evaluation of when it is safe for a concussion patient to return to the field is the neurocognitive baseline test. Thousands of school districts are having their older athletes — there is no reliable test for a 10-year-old, for example — take the computerized tests before they begin a season.

The tests, which measure reaction time, learning and memory skills, and how quickly a person thinks and solves problems, are stored for future use. If an athlete sustains a head injury, the preseason test can be used to assess whether the athlete's cognitive function has been altered. More important, weeks after a concussion, the test can help measure whether the athlete still has a cognitive deficit.

However, it is not a concussion test. In addition, concussion specialists do not recommend retaking the baseline test soon after a head injury because it can exacerbate concussion symptoms. It is also not meant to be the only test that determines whether an athlete is ready to play again.

"It is not a red-light, green-light test," said Alex Taylor, a neuropsychologist at Boston Children's Hospital who works with patients from the concussion clinic. "That is where people get sidetracked. It does not determine who is completely recovered. It is one of the tools for doing that."

Inside the Boston clinics, in consult, a team of neurologists, sports medicine and rehabilitation specialists, physical therapists, psychologists and psychiatrists may determine a recommended course for a single patient.

But the acknowledged subjective nature of this multifaceted process often leads to awkward office meetings among doctors, patients and parents. Put a high school state playoff game or a major recruiting showcase in the immediate future of a promising athlete whose concussion occurred three weeks ago — but has not healed sufficiently, according to the doctors — and the discussion can become contentious.

"People argue with you, especially if it's a high-level athlete who is playing on three different soccer teams and the family feels they've invested years in an upcoming opportunity and now we're getting in the way," Panis said. "But you know, I've also had the kid trying to talk me into playing and had mom in the corner shaking her head and saying: 'No, he's not himself yet. Don't let him.' Parents know their kids best."

Panis routinely declines to sign the forms required by Massachusetts law for a return to competition, even if he knows some patients just take the forms elsewhere.

"You can always find a doctor to agree with you," he said.

Other patients barred from playing for their schools suit up instead for their travel teams, which are not required to abide by state youth sports concussion laws.

Panis has treated young athletes who had nine concussions and were still playing.

"They're teenagers," he said. "They have one or two and keep going without much of a problem until it catches up with them."

Brian Lilja, a patient at Boston Children's Hospital's concussion clinic and a junior who played football and lacrosse for Methuen High School outside Boston, recalls sustaining what he now knows was a concussion as a freshman football player. He probably had a second concussion later that season. He kept playing.

"The players are bigger in high school and they hit harder; I didn't really worry about it or care," Lilja said in February. "I stayed in."

Then, playing lacrosse last spring, he sustained a third concussion.

"This time, he couldn't have possibly played anything —he had a hard time getting out of bed," his mother, Jennifer Lilja, said. "The personality change was scary. He was just so spacey. Studying gave him headaches. Here was a big, 6-foot-2 kid not being able to do much of anything.

"Eventually, he was very depressed. It was heart-breaking seeing all the effects of something we just didn't understand."

Seven months after Brian Lilja's last concussion, his symptoms subsided enough that he started to help coach Methuen's junior varsity lacrosse team. With a gradual schedule laid out by the clinic's doctors, he resumed a normal classroom workload.

"I read every story about concussions in the N.F.L. and N.H.L., and I tell my friends and other athletes everything I've learned," Lilja said. "I wish I knew what I know now; I would have rested my brain after my first concussion."

CLINICS' BOTTOM LINES

The nationwide proliferation of youth sports clinics is a reaction to a health care demand. But are the clinics also profit centers?

Dr. Peter Greenspan, the vice chairman of the pediatrics department at Massachusetts General Hospital and medical director of MassGeneral Hospital for Children, said of his clinic: "We're happy if we break even. It does not produce revenue."

Meehan, of Boston Children's Hospital, responded similarly, saying that if the clinic was good for business, it was principally because of the good will it brought the institution.

Interviews with directors of youth concussion clinics nationwide produced a consensus that the clinics were not significant moneymakers because they were not procedure driven, meaning that they do not typically lead to expensive imaging tests or operations. Instead, they tie up doctors in lengthy, multifaceted patient consultations.

But Michael Bergeron, the executive director of the National Youth Sports Health and Safety Institute, offered an additional perspective. Bergeron agreed that the clinics do not usually lead to costly procedures, but he said the volume of patients they attracted to an institution or an individual practice could have residual benefits that boosted the bottom line.

"Concussion clinics might be seen as a loss leader for the halo effect they bring the institution," Bergeron said. "People recognize you as an authority offering a timely service that is very much in the news. It might make them consider you for other treatments, too. It's another dimension to promote on your Web site. It's an opportunity to lift your profile."

Notice of the Boston clinics is not hard to find on their hospital Web sites, but they have not otherwise been marketed aggressively. Trying to find them at the hospitals can be somewhat challenging because they are tucked inside larger, more established sports medicine wings.

Most clinic patients go to the clinics because they are referred by their pediatricians, their primary care physicians or the doctors attending to them during an emergency room visit. Emergency room visits by children and adolescents with brain injuries have increased by more than 60 percent in the past eight years, according to the federal Centers for Disease Control and Prevention.

"Parents are better informed and they want these injuries better managed, which is the right reaction," said Kevin Guskiewicz, the founding director of the Matthew Gfeller Sport-Related Traumatic Brain Injury Research Center at the University of North Carolina. "So I'm not surprised there are all these concussion clinics sprouting up to treat their kids. Time will tell if it is a novelty. What happens when the heightened awareness and fear subsides?"

Some concussion specialists working at clinics said they believed the facilities would be more prevalent in 5 or 10 years, with a clinic perhaps located near every medium-size city in the country.

"I think that's pretty likely," O'Brien, of the Boston Children's Hospital clinic, said. "Although I do think, as pediatricians and primary care providers get more continuing medical education about concussions, they will become more comfortable and adept with treating them in their office.

"Clinics like ours may be the places for the more complex cases."

O'Brien said nearly half of the current cases at the clinic would be classified as nonstandard or complex.

"And that's 200 cases a month in one clinic in one city," he said.

If the widespread anxiety about concussions is diminished in time, if the frenzy that doctors describe abates, there could be other outcomes as well, like a better understanding that a concussion in a school-age athlete is not necessarily a pathway to the kind of dementia found in some aging N.F.L. players.

"Too often these days, I see moms and dads who are so worried about a kid's concussion or so worried about a second concussion that they discourage their kid from playing their sports," Meehan said. "That's the worst thing they can do. A concussion is a problem and a serious one, but at the same time, obesity and sedentary lifestyles are having a much greater impact on society. The worst thing we could do is make kids less active."

Ginsburg, the Massachusetts General psychologist, who has written a book about youth sports, speaks frequently at schools and likes to poll the student audiences on various issues. One recent weekday at the clinic, staff members convened in a conference room for lunch.

"I was at an elementary school recently," Ginsburg told the group. "I interviewed the students and asked them to name the No. 1 thing they were afraid of. They all started talking about concussions."

The room went silent.

"People talk about the future of concussion management," Ginsburg said. "In 10 years, if I go back to that elementary school and ask the kids what they're afraid of, I really hope concussions aren't the first thing that comes to mind."

1. Do you believe youth sports clinic administrators when they say they do not turn a profit? Why or why not?

EXCERPT FROM "SPORTS-RELATED CONCUSSIONS AND TRAUMATIC BRAIN INJURIES: RESEARCH ROUNDUP," FROM *JOURNALIST'S RESOURCE*, OCTOBER 22, 2014

The issue of concussions in sports has attracted considerable media coverage in recent years. Understandably, the early focus was on professional football, a game built around high-speed, full contact between heavy, powerful players, but the scope of reporting and research has expanded widely to include sports at every level.

A pioneer of reporting in this field was Alan Schwarz of the *New York Times*; his work highlighted the history of concussions and their consequences in the NFL. The league has responded by banning some high-risk hits, and also aggressively investigated a "bounty pools" scandal that involved a team paying bonuses to players who injured opponents. (Similar behavior has even turned up in a Pop Warner youth league.) Retired players continue to pursue legal action and raise awareness of the issue, particularly with cases of former players suffering from early-onset dementia that can result from repeated brain trauma. In January 2013, the National Institutes of Health concluded that the former NFL linebacker Junior Seau, who committed suicide in May 2012, had been suffering from a degenerative brain disease.

Ice hockey is another rough, physical sport that takes a high toll. NHL all-star player Sidney Crosby was out for the better part of a year, beginning in 2010, because of a severe concussion. The long-term consequences of such injuries can be dire: A post-mortem of NHL "enforcer" Derek Boogaard, who died in May 2011, determined that he suffered from chronic traumatic encephalopathy, a progressive degenerative disease directly linked to repeated brain injuries.

Even professional sports that aren't designed around physical contact between players can result in concussions. During the National Basketball Association 2012 Finals, Oklahoma City star James Harden suffered one just before the beginning of the playoffs. In Major League Baseball, concussions are known to have helped end the careers of Mike Matheny (now the manager of the St. Louis Cardinals) and Corey Koskie; they also cost Minnesota Twins star Justin Morneau the better part of a season of play. The league instituted a disabled list for players with concussions in 2011 and continues to work on the issue.

Concussion risk starts at the youth level, in football and ice hockey as well as baseball, soccer, boxing, gymnastics, horseback riding, skiing and cycling — any sport with potential for hard contact. The best available evidence continues to raise questions about whether schools and teams are doing enough. Two 2014 studies in *The American Journal of Sports Medicine* suggest as much: One study, which was based on a survey of 1066 collegiate institutions, concludes that "although a large majority of respondents indicated that their school has a concussion management plan, improvement is needed." Another paper about protective equipment at the high school level found that among 2081 players enrolled during the 2012-13 football seasons, some 206 (9%) sustained a total of 211 concussions. That study notes that, regardless of the type and brand of protective equipment, incidence of concussion remains the same — suggesting that it is the nature of on-field play that remains at issue. Still, because of specific concerns over youth football, Virginia Tech and Wake Forest have started a ratings system for helmets.

According to the Centers for Disease Control and Prevention, U.S. emergency departments annually treat an average of 173,285 sports- and recreation-related traumatic brain injuries among children and adolescents. Such emergency visits have increased 60% over the past decade; in 2009 alone, there were 248,418 such cases.

New research from Harvard, Dartmouth, Brown and Virginia Tech has called into question whether current diagnostic techniques are adequate. In addition, the long-term effects of head injury are only partially understood. The Boston University Center for Traumatic Encephalopathy, which received a $1 million donation from the NFL in 2010, continues to examine the brains of deceased athletes to research and compile case studies on the long-term effects of concussions; the center also conducts other inquiries and publishes academic studies in this evolving field.

Finally, a 2014 study published in the journal of *Medicine & Science in Sports & Exercise* provides new evidence that high school athletes may be returning to the field too early after suffering a concussion.

1. Are you surprised by the accusation included in this round-up that some youth leagues awarded students "bonuses" for injuring opponents? Why or why not?

"ARE PARENTS MORALLY OBLIGATED TO FORBID THEIR KIDS FROM PLAYING FOOTBALL?", BY KATHLEEN BACHYNSKI, FROM *THE CONVERSATION*, JUNE 2, 2015

In March 2015, San Francisco 49ers linebacker Chris Borland shocked football fans when he announced his decision to retire after just one season in the NFL.

He explained that he was concerned over the long-term health hazards of football-related head trauma, and journalists and media personalities covered the story extensively.

Some observers asked if Borland's retirement might prove the "beginning of the end" for the NFL, while others suggested that the league would remain unchanged.

But looking beyond the NFL, might Borland's decision – along with the ever-growing body of evidence on football-related concussions and brain injuries – influence football at the youth level? With professional athletes serving as role models to children aspiring to follow in their footsteps, the decisions of popular sports stars can often have a major impact on the safety of youth athletes.

Parents generally have final say over the activities their kids participate in. Should they follow the lead of Borland, and forbid their children from playing football? Unfortunately, there's no simple answer. Instead, a host of issues – cultural, social and physical – need to be weighed.

LEADING BY EXAMPLE

In ice hockey, the decision of all-star NHL goalie Jacques Plante to begin wearing a face mask quite literally changed the face of the game.

181

In the 1950s, hockey goalies didn't wear face masks. Some observers at the time argued that parents who allowed their children to play hockey without proper equipment were violating their duty to protect their kids. However, despite these concerns – and the sport's inherent violence – wearing head protection was generally regarded as a sign of cowardice.

Plante's bold move (and success on the ice) helped challenge a prevailing culture in which wearing face protection was frowned upon. Others soon followed his lead: both professional and amateur hockey goalies adopted face masks, an innovation that prevented countless injuries (while saving untold numbers of teeth!).

PROTECTION IS AT THE HEART OF PARENTING

Clearly, the actions of prominent players within a sport can have a huge influence. However, Plante didn't decide to *stop* playing ice hockey; he simply chose to wear more protective equipment.

So what happens when a young, healthy star like Chris Borland walks away from a popular sport entirely? With Borland's decision, how should parents respond on behalf of their children?

Asking if and when tackle football is appropriate for children raises fundamental ethical challenges. As a professional adult athlete, Borland can choose to walk away from football if he deems the sport too risky.

But in general, parents must make these decisions for their children. It's both common sense and scientific fact: children don't possess the full range of emotional and cognitive abilities to make judgments about what's in their own best interest.

Parents, then, have a moral obligation to protect their child's health and welfare.

WEIGHING THE RISKS WITH THE BENEFITS

On the other hand, virtually *all* childhood activities offer both health risks and benefits. So the question becomes: how much risk is too much? How great should the potential benefits be in order to outweigh the potential risks? And how can parents make judgments when the risks and benefits are uncertain?

These are complicated questions, especially when it comes to a sport as beloved and culturally important as American football.

For many parents, the potential long-term risk of head trauma is not the only factor they consider when signing their children up to play football. They are also considering the benefit of physical activity. Perhaps even more importantly, there are the social, emotional and mental health benefits of playing team sports. Finally, football plays a uniquely prominent role in the social life of many American schools and communities.

Sports Illustrated writer Greg Bedard recently noted that football "remains a pillar of community, a tie that binds." A number of parents cherish the social skills, bonding and connection to the larger community that participation in such a sport can provide for their children.

Many people also believe that at least some of the violence inherent to football is, in itself, a benefit. They argue that children and adolescents – particularly boys – are inherently aggressive, that football provides a relatively healthy outlet for that aggression.

As writer Jonathan Chait asserted, "Football channels boys' chauvinistic belligerence into supervised forms, shapes them within boundaries, and gives them positive meaning."

Yet the scientific evidence for some of these claims is slim. It's not clear, for example, that tackling each other on the football field is the only (or best) outlet for high-energy adolescents. And alternative sports or other activities such as music or theater can teach children social skills.

WHAT THE RESEARCH DOES – AND DOESN'T – SAY

At the same time, there's also a dearth of scientific evidence showing long-term health risks associated with youth football. The most recent research indicates that repetitive hits to the head (even if the hits do not cause concussions) can alter the brains of high school football players.

Yet what these changes mean for these adolescents' *long-term* health is still unknown. No one has yet done a study to see if youth football players who stop playing upon reaching high school or college are more likely to develop dementia or other diseases later in life.

In 2014, the NFL acknowledged that nearly one-third of its players would go on to develop long-term cognitive problems, but the comparable risk for children who played in middle or high school is unknown. Many factors – the speed and age of the players, the magnitude of the hits – make youth football quite different from the professional game.

In the meantime, some researchers have suggested eliminating high-impact drills for youth players during practice. Yet such harm reduction strategies have not yet been evaluated to see if they protect players' long-term health.

Unfortunately, parents cannot wait for scientists to reach a clearer understanding of the exact risks of youth football.

They have to make decisions for their children in the context of significant uncertainty about just how dangerous – and how beneficial – football may be.

Knowing that there may be significant risks and that children are vulnerable, perhaps parents should err on the side of caution and limit their children's participation in football. Certainly, the risk of cognitive impairment should be weighed differently from the risk of arthritis or lower back pain.

Nonetheless, balancing the advantages of a more cautious approach with its disadvantanges – potentially depriving children of a fun and valued activity – is no easy matter. There may be no single right answer, but parents must carefully consider what we know about football and children's health, and what remains to be learned.

1. How do you weigh in on this? If parents have an ethical obligation to protect their children, should they not permit them to play high-contact sports like football if they risk serious injury?

CHAPTER 6

WHAT THE PUBLIC SAYS

A national health poll, conducted in late 2015, revealed how Americans presently feel about head injuries in sports. It is simple. They want teams, organizations, leagues and coaches to do a better job protecting the players whether they are all-star veteran hockey players or little children playing in pee-wee football leagues.

"There's definitely an increase in concern for players at all levels," said Dr. Sharief Taraman, a pediatric neurologist at Children's Hospital of Orange County, California. "Although it started with NFL players having these tragic outcomes, it's trickled down to even the pediatric level."

People who responded to the poll said that there should be a standardized test and protocol to deal with head injuries and to determine the severity. They also – fans and non-sports fans alike – said that anyone suffering from a head injury should not be allowed to play unless they are cleared medically.

An interesting side note to the poll is that more than 80 percent of those who responded said that those playing the games know what the risks are because they are so widely known and have accepted those risks.

On the other side of that, several famous former or current football players have said publicly that they would never let their children play football.

"MOVIE AS GAME-CHANGER: OPINIONS VARY ON HOW 'CONCUSSION' MAY OR MAY NOT AFFECT THE NFL," FROM *PT IN MOTION NEWS*, DECEMBER 28, 2015

Concussion has been released—and with it, a wave of opinions on whether the film about chronic traumatic encephalopathy (CTE) among National Football League (NFL) players will make a difference in how the league, and society at large, view sports that involve high impact body contact.

The movie, which opened on December 25, stars Will Smith as forensic pathologist Bennett Omalu and chronicles Omalu's battle with the NFL to bring attention to CTE and its relationship to repeated head injury.

And while there were plenty of reviews of the movie itself, even more media attention was focused on what the film had to say about the NFL, the sport of football, America's passion for the game, and the chances that a big-budget movie would spark any meaningful change that would reduce injury. Here's a quick rundown of some of the reactions published recently.

- "CTE, and the prevalence of the disease among the young, however, has given [the NFL] a PR nightmare. And Concussion is likely to worsen the public's perception of the game." Newsweek: "Concussion: Can a Will Smith Movie Change the Way America Views Football?"
- "Many of our retired gridiron heroes have come forward to say they have some form of brain damage from their glory days. Joe Namath, Brett Favre, Tony Dorsett, Terry Bradshaw, Harry Carson, the list goes on and it will continue to grow. I have no pity for them." Chicago Tribune: "NFL Players, Owners, and Fans All to Blame for Concussion Danger" (opinion from columnist Jerry Davich)
- "[CBS Philadelphia sports commentator Jeff] Roe saw the film with me and questioned why, after seeing it, I was rushing home to see the Eagles. My response was I thought the players were now informed fully of the risks and didn't feel that I was morally shaky by enjoying such a violent game." CBS Philadelphia review: "Concussion Movie Will Not Cripple the NFL"
- "But Concussion may actually make a difference because it doesn't require government action or even civilian action. All civilians have to do to voice their opposition is to not watch football and not play football." *Forbes* magazine: "Why Will Smith's 'Concussion' May Actually Impact the NFL"
- "In a film with so little interest in gray areas, the bad guy becomes everyone who isn't the good guys, which leads us to Concussion's most troubling villain: us. For a movie that's ostensibly about

how awful football is, Concussion sure has a lot of nice things to say about football." Slate: "Hands to the Face: The Woeful 'Concussion' Fails to Hold the NFL—or Anyone—Accountable for the CTE Crisis"

- "Parents and players now know the warning signs [of CTE]. It does not mean that football will ever go away. As noted in the film, the NFL owns a day of the week. And it now stretches its tentacles to Thursday nights, Monday nights, and the occasional Saturday playoff game." Orlando Sentinel: "Brain Science Slowly Beaten Into NFL Owners' Heads in 'Concussion'" (opinion from columnist George Diaz)

- "Any activity which results in repeated blows to the head has the risk of causing brain damage. Once you know the risk involved in something, what's the first thing you do? Protect the children from it." Quote from Bennett Omalu in the Guardian: "Doctor Who Fought NFL Says 'No Equipment Can Prevent' Such Injuries"

- "We have a grandson who plays. He's 7. After seeing this movie, I should probably go call his parents and say he shouldn't play anymore. But I can't do that. Isn't that awful? I'd rather roll the dice." Quote from Taz Anderson, former NFL player, in Sports Illustrated: 'Paid to Give Concussions' (Screening of 'Concussion' with 70 former NFL players)

- Physical therapists have a critical role in concussion prevention and management. APTA offers multiple resources on concussion, which include a Traumatic Brain Injury webpage, and a clinical summary on concussion available for free to members on PTNow. The association also offers a patient-focused Physical Therapist's Guide to Concussion on APTA's MoveForwardPT.com consumer website. Continuing education offerings from APTA include the prerecorded webinar "Managing Concussions With an Interprofessional Team" and the online course "Concussion and the Postconcussive Syndrome," both available through the APTA Learning Center.

1. Do you think movies like *Concussion* can be game-changers in the public's perception of the risks involved in minors playing high-contact sports?

"FACING THE CONCUSSION RISKS OF YOUTH FOOTBALL," BY KATHLEEN E. BACHYNSKI AND DANIEL S. GOLDBERG, FROM THE PHILADELPHIA MEDIA NETWORK, SEPTEMBER 26, 2014

After years of denying the link between football and brain disease, this month the National Football League's own experts calculated that nearly one third of its players will go on to develop long-term cognitive problems after retirement. The league's new stance might help shift public perceptions of football's extraordinary risks to professional players' brains. From a public health perspective, examining the sport's impact on millions of youth players is of even greater importance.

Children as young as seven and eight continue to play tackle football across the United States in far greater numbers than NFL stars. Accumulating evidence suggests that the repeated collisions inherent in the youth sport may cause significant harm. The players might be smaller, but the hits are still dangerous. Researchers have found that nine-twelve year olds can experience head impacts of a similar magnitude to those that occur in high school and college football. Furthermore, because children's brains are still developing and because they have weaker necks than adults, they may be more vulnerable to brain trauma.

Why do parents allow their children to participate in a sport that poses significant risks to developing brains? One reason is that organizers of youth football leagues portray the youth game as much safer than the professional game. The Pop Warner website, for example, states that there is "an absence of catastrophic head and neck injuries and disruptive joint injuries found at higher levels" in their league. Such assertions seem to discount the potential severity of concussions, which are common in youth football and can have major short-term and long-term consequences. Parents may not fully appreciate the risks associated with football head injuries. A recent study of over three hundred football parents found that most did not realize that a concussion is considered a mild traumatic brain injury, or that a direct blow to the head is not necessary for a concussion to occur. (A two-page fact sheet with danger signs and symptoms of concussions is here.)

Yet even if parents acknowledge that concussions are a significant injury, most people believe that strategies such as improved helmets, return-to-play guidelines, and "safer" tackling techniques can help significantly reduce the risks of concussion. Indeed, the NFL has helped promote this prevailing view, most notably with its "Heads Up Football" partnership with youth leagues, intended to teach proper tackling techniques to children.

There is no evidence that the "Heads Up Football" program reduces the risk of concussion or of long-term brain damage: As former Denver Broncos tight end Nate Jackson has observed, no matter what tackling technique children use, "you can't remove the head from play in the football field."

Unfortunately, improved helmet design is not a silver bullet either. Although helmets are very effective in preventing catastrophic head injuries such as skull fractures, they are not designed to prevent concussions. Even the best designed helmet cannot prevent the forces that occur when the head rotates on the neck. Kevin Walter of the American Academy of Pediatrics' Council on Sports Medicine and Fitness recently stated that currently, "no protective equipment can prevent concussion."

Although education, training, and improved equipment are all worth encouraging, they do not change the fundamental risks of the sport. Football is a contact game in which repeated full-body collisions place players' brains at risk of chronic trauma. We must acknowledge that the risk of head injuries is inherent to tackle football, even at the youth level, and will remain significant even with new equipment designs or the best tackling techniques.

We need to ask different questions. At what point are the risks of head injuries so high or severe that even fully informed parents should not be permitted to let their children to play? And at what age can players consent to the risk of brain trauma and the elevated risks of neurological diseases later in life?

These are complex ethical issues that involve not only examining the latest concussion research, but also our values and beliefs about how much risk is appropriate for children. Of course, children should be encouraged to play and lead active lives, and experiencing some amount of risk in childhood is inevitable. But how much risk is too much?

Addressing this question will require a robust public discussion involving parents, coaches, school administrators, fans, trainers, physicians, sporting goods manufacturers, and the players themselves. While children certainly benefit from participation in team sports, it remains a question whether other sports can offer those same benefits while posing less risk of brain injury than tackle football. Do the risks of America's most popular sport outweigh its benefits for young children?

1. How would you answer this last question: Do the risks of America's most popular sport outweigh its benefits for young children?

"BARROW CONCUSSION NETWORK BUILT TO PROTECT ARIZONA HIGH SCHOOL ATHLETES," BY MICHAEL NOWELS, FROM *CRONKITE NEWS*, APRIL 28, 2015

Kyle Janes plays linebacker for Phoenix Christian High School. He suffered a concussion on the field this year. But the injury came in a less expected spot: the baseball diamond.

"I backhanded it and it hit off my glove, hit me right here in my forehead," said the freshman shortstop, pointing to the middle of his brow.

Janes picked up the ball and threw it to first, but the damage was already done.

Phoenix Christian athletic trainer Dayna Tierney noticed Janes looked disoriented, administered a concussion test and determined Janes needed to come out of the game.

Janes saw Dr. Kareem Shaarawy at St. Joseph's Hospital and Medical Center, who assessed his injury and held him out of baseball for two weeks.

Shaarawy advised Janes to attend half days of school for the week after his injury.

Janes returned to Shaarawy's office and continued to show concussion symptoms on the first visit. It wasn't until his next visit that he was given the all-clear to return to play.

He may not recognize it, but Janes participated in the Barrow Concussion Network's three-pronged strategy to combat concussion in athletes.

The network is a collection of partners in Arizona devoted to educating, diagnosing and treating athletes from grade school through the professional ranks.

It is made up of the Barrow Neurological Institute, the Arizona Interscholastic Association, A.T. Still University, the Brain Injury Alliance of Arizona, the Arizona Cardinals and Arizona State University. Each entity fulfills a slightly different role within the network, making up one of the most comprehensive concussion-based groups in the nation.

EDUCATION: BARROW BRAINBOOK

Prior to the football season, Janes and his team completed Barrow Brainbook, a 50-minute educational course about issues surrounding concussion. The course mimics social media, and students can agree or disagree with posts and comments made by characters with the goal of answering in the most brain-healthy way.

"Every single athlete in the state of Arizona is required to take this before they step onto the field, onto the court, into the water," said Dr. Javier Cárdenas, who spearheads the project as the director of the Concussion and Brain Injury Center at Barrow. "We've had over a quarter million kids complete this education."

Students must pass with a score of at least 85 percent before they receive a certificate verifying that they have completed the course. They must show their coaches the certificate to participate with their team.

Arizona State graduate students in educational technology helped Barrow develop Brainbook in 2011.

The course is about more than avoiding concussion.

"We want them, if they think they have a concussion or if they feel like they have concussion symptoms, to report it to their coach, to their parent, to their athletic trainer or to another adult," said Tamara McLeod, the director of A.T. Still's athletic training program. "I think a lot of them don't understand that it can affect their schooling."

McLeod used the analogy of a knee injury – it's obvious to students and those around them that even once the knee brace comes off, there's still work to be done.

"Unlike the example, post-surgery in a brace, a concussed athlete normally looks normal. They look fine, they act fine for the most part and yeah, they want to go back to play," McLeod said.

Kim Rodgers, the athletic trainer at Mountain Ridge High School and an A.T. Still graduate, stressed the importance of trainers interacting with and educating families at parents' activities throughout the season. She explains to parents the different elements of the network so they understand the system working to protect their children.

"It gives the whole family definitely a comfort level," she said.

The theme of education even extends to A.T. Still. McLeod's program provides graduate students as athletic trainers for some area high schools. Many graduates of the program work at Arizona high schools and community colleges, according to McLeod, but the program has also worked to reach schools without direct affiliations to A.T. Still.

One A.T. Still graduate student working in the field is Tierney.

Tierney, Rodgers and all other Arizona high school athletic trainers administer a baseline test at the beginning of the year called ImPACT (Immediate Post-Concussion Assessment and Cognitive Testing). Neither Tierney nor Rodgers uses ImPACT for immediate assessment, though. Rather, they and the doctors they partner with use it to determine if an athlete is ready to return to play after a concussion.

The NFL and NHL both use ImPACT, which measures concussion symptoms on a Likert scale of 1-7 and tests various cognitive functions, including different types of matching and memory. The network provides ImPACT to all the schools in the state at no cost.

Tierney said there's a different test athletic trainers use to diagnose concussion on the sidelines, the test she used to diagnose Janes.

"The one we mainly use is called the SCAT 3, Tierney said, referencing the third edition of the Sport Concussion Assessment Tool. "It has about five different sections: It tests memory, cognition, recall and balance and motor function as well."

The athletes at Phoenix Christian already know what's probably coming if Tierney takes out the SCAT.

"My kids know me well enough now to know that if I'm testing them for a concussion, if we're already to that point, more than likely they're concussed," she said. "Of course, they're disappointed but I think most of them are feeling so cruddy at that point that they're like, 'Yeah, I want to go home and sleep so that's fine with me.'"

Some athletic trainers also use Sway, a smartphone application that measures balance, to get a better idea of the athlete's condition.

Rodgers said she gives parents of concussed athletes the option of going to urgent care. She always answers questions and provides them a handout on concussion from the Centers for Disease Control and Prevention.

After sideline diagnosis, there's still the issue of sending the athlete to a neurologist to determine the severity of the injury and map out a plan of action for both academics and athletics.

TREATMENT: PATIENCE IS A VIRTUE

Tierney said the neurologist dictates the recovery schedule for the athlete. That timeline not only approaches time away from contact sports but also time away from physical activity in general. It often includes missing some classes.

Cárdenas said the network has five concussion specialists available for consultation, whether in their office or sometimes through telemedicine, a Skype-style format that allows the doctor to assess the patient remotely.

Even with the decreased activity of half days at school, Janes felt the effects of his head injury.

"I remember in computer class, I'd be looking at the screen and then after five minutes my head would start hurting and I couldn't focus and so I had to like close my eyes for a little bit," he said. "It was kind of tough the first week but the second week was a whole lot better."

McLeod, Rodgers and Tierney all stressed the importance of cognitive rest when recovering from a concussion.

"The next step is making sure that teachers under-stand that the concussion can result in certain symptoms and sometimes some basic accommodations might need to take place in the classroom on a temporary basis," McLeod said.

After some rest, students return to class incremen-tally, ramping back up to their normal workload. McLeod said students should always return to the classroom before returning to their sport. Tierney said she tries to relay the importance of long-term brain health to the students to help them be patient.

"You've got to kind of take it out of the context of today and think kind of down the line because we don't want it to cause other issues," she said.

McLeod agrees.

"I think some of the best role models are those that have not rushed back to play in the professional ranks," she said. McLeod singled out Pittsburgh Penguins super-star Sidney Crosby, who missed the second half of the 2011-12 season and the beginning of the 2012-13 campaign after suffering a concussion in the Winter Classic on Jan. 1, 2012.

The process takes the decision of returning away from the athlete, coach and parent and puts that respon-sibility in the hands of those with the medical back-ground to assess the athlete's condition: athletic trainers and neurologists.

Janes said he and his father were anxious to get him back on the field as quickly as possible, but it was worth the wait to be sure he was healthy.

"I didn't like it at all but I was cheering on my team and wishing the best for them," he said. "Actually,

I think they won all the games that I was out so I was happy for them."

The athletic trainer keeps an eye on the student and the doctor consults frequently with the student until the doctor determines it is time to retest using ImPACT.

Janes knew he was in good hands after taking the test a second time. He scored higher than he did on his baseline test in the fall.

He's back playing shortstop and pitching for the Cougars after a successful trip through the Barrow Concussion Network.

1. Do you think the Barrow Concussion Network is a successful way of treating concussions for minors playing high-contact sports? Why or why not?

"SOCCER CONCUSSIONS STRESS VALUE OF HEADGEAR," BY JAKUB RUDNIK, FROM THE *REDLINE PROJECT*, NOVEMBER 27, 2013

In the spring of 2010, the day before his high school graduation, Graham Wallace was playing basketball with friends and was struck with a ball in the head.

"It wasn't even hard," he said.

That afternoon during graduation practice, however, Wallace felt dizzy and light-headed and was taken to a local hospital. It was his fourth concussion, with the previous three all a result of playing soccer.

Soccer may not have the same amount of contact or level of physicality as football, but the sport has one of the highest concussion rates in all of sports. Among collegiate sports, women's soccer was found to have the highest rate of concussions, along with men's lacrosse. (Journal of Athletic Training 2003) Women's soccer also comprises the second-highest percentage of total concussions, behind men's football. (The American Journal of Sports Medicine 2012)

While soccer players do repeatedly use their heads to pass the ball during games and practice, that is the least common way for them to sustain a concussion. More often it occurs from an elbow during a challenge for a header, a goalkeeper getting kicked or kneed in the head or diving into a goalpost, or a player unexpectedly getting hit in the head with the ball. (F-MARC) It is estimated that between 4 percent to 20 percent of soccer injuries are head injuries. (The Sport Journal 2009)

YOUTH SOCCER

Wallace sustained his first concussion in 5th grade during an indoor soccer tournament. During a routine save he bobbled the ball and an opposing player kneed him in the head.

"One of my friends' dads was taping the game so I've watched the hit—it was pretty nasty," he said.

Concussions in youth soccer like Wallace's are not uncommon. According to a study by Northern Kentucky University, the Center for Disease Control and Prevention reported "Doctors treat more than 200,000 children annually for soccer-related injuries including concussions." (The Sport Journal 2009)

Younger athletes are not only at a higher risk for concussions, there is evidence that they experience more severe symptoms than their older counterparts. High school soccer players performed worse on verbal, visual and memory Post-Concussion Assessments than college players. They also recovered at a slower rate. (The American Journal of Sports Medicine 2012) Additionally, female athletes performed worse on the visual Assessment and reported more symptoms than their male counterparts.

In an effort to reduce concussions among young players, there has been a call by some to ban headers until players are old enough to have more developed brains and are skilled enough to properly execute headers. Dr. Bob Cantu, chairman of the surgery division and the director of sports medicine at Emerson Hospital in Concord, Massachusetts, has been cited by NBC Sports calling for a ban on heading for players 14-and-under.

NCAA RAISES AWARENESS FOR COLLEGE ATHLETES

Eric Foster, an Alma College assistant coach and a former Alma College player himself, had his second concussion as a freshman at the Michigan school in 2008 (the first was not soccer related).

"It was late October or early November so the ground was frozen and hard. The opposing player ran right through me and I hit the back of my head on the ground", said Foster. He said he has no recollection of the next five minutes.

I was told that I got up and tried to run, but I couldn't stand upright. The other coach had to call over the trainer. He [the trainer] told me later that I was talking and not making sense—it was like I was super drunk."

Foster said that at that time the NCAA did not require a sideline test before reentering a game after experiencing concussion-like symptoms. "All I had to do [to reenter] was jog around the field once. He asked if I was dizzy. I just lied and told him I wasn't."

The NCAA and individual universities have made it a point in recent years to make athletes more aware of concussion syndromes and long-term effects. Both DePaul University and Northwestern University display concussion policies and resources on their athletic department websites.

The NCAA is now a driving force behind concussion awareness among young athletes. A "Concussions" menu is one of the six options within "Health and Safety" on the NCAA website. Within the site athletes can find additional concussion resources and news articles about concussion studies. Additionally, the NCAA has concussion posters for men and women to be posted in training facilities and locker rooms as well as a video for athlete awareness.

Jeff Carrico, assistant director of sports medicine at DePaul, said in an email interview that the treatment of concussions by the school's training staff has not changed.

"The only thing that has changed is that we are obtaining more resources from organizations like the NCAA Health and Safety committee and the National Athletic Trainers Association on how to recognize, prevent, and care for concussions," he wrote.

FIFA'S RESEARCH

FIFA, the international governing body of soccer, is also raising awareness for concussions while conducting research of its own. On its website it provides resources for concussion awareness among young athletes as well as a concussion cheat sheet for coaches and trainers.

Among its own athletes, FIFA has conducted studies of both men's and women's competitions in order to identify causes of soccer concussion, potential gender disparity and the safety of heading a soccer ball. A study identified aerial challenges as the cause of more than half of soccer concussions, while saying that "the accelerations heading causes to the head of a player are below the level associated with brain injury." (F-MARC) In other words, there is not enough force when heading a soccer ball to cause a concussion.

The organization has made a rule change to help minimize concussions in international soccer. Prior to the 2006 World Cup it made an amendment to the Laws of the Game calling for red cards (an automatic ejection and loss of player for the team) in cases of elbowing to the head. FIFA reported fewer concussions in 2006 than in previous World Cups.

FIFA also hosted a two-day concussion conference in Zurich, Switzerland on Oct. 30-31, 2012. FIFA was joined by the International Ice Hockey Federation, the International Olympic Committee and the International Rugby Board. Results of the conference will be published in the future.

INJURIES AMONG PROFESSIONAL ATHLETES

Likely the most famous soccer concussion of all-time happened on Oct. 14, 2006 to Chelsea FC (and Czech Republic national team) goalkeeper Petr Čech. In the first minute of the Chelsea/Reading FC match, Čech was kneed in the head by midfielder Stephen Hunt.

Čech had skull fractures and a severe concussion. In a 2009 interview with Daily Mail, Čech said "At the beginning I had difficulty speaking. The words came out all wrong. I'd have terrible headaches."

When he made his return in January, Čech wore protective headgear to cushion future impact. While many studies doubt the value of soccer headgear for field players heading a ball, for an often defenseless goalkeeper the added protection has much more obvious value. After a 2011 game against Fulham (and another concussion), Čech told The Telegraph the helmet prevented a second serious brain injury.

In 2011, Logan Pause of the Chicago Fire suffered a concussion on an unexpected header. In a Chicago Tribune article Pause said that it was not until after the game that he felt the effects of the concussion, "After the game and the next three days, I had some pretty bad headaches." Like Čech, Pause returned from injury with a rugby-style helmet to offer him protection.

In January 2012, Major League Soccer hosted a symposium for team athletic trainers and physicians to update concussion protocol. Changing the rules for re-entering a game after experiencing concussion-like symptoms will help prevent players from staying in a game like Pause after suffering a concussion.

PROTECTIVE HEAD GEAR

After his fourth concussion, Wallace also began to wear protective headgear at the request of his parents and doctors, as well as for his own safety. Over two years later and Wallace has just finished his third season playing varsity soccer at Division III Alma College in Michigan. Since he began wearing the headgear after his high school graduation he has not suffered another concussion.

While evidence for the value of protective headgear has grown, there has not always support for the headgear. The U.S. Soccer Federation allows protective headgear, but does not endorse it. In fact, the Federation website has not updated its stance on headgear since 2005.

Soccer officials also worry that endorsing headgear could hurt the future of the game. It could scare parents away from signing their children up to play.

The headgear was originally thought to be protection from injuries caused during intentional heading of the ball, which has proved to be the least common cause of soccer concussions. Headgear has been proven to reduce impact of heading a soccer ball (Journal of Athletic Training 2003), but if that is not a primary cause of soccer concussions, then where is the value?

In recent years, there has been more evidence that headgear reduces soccer concussions as a whole. In a study of soccer players age 12-17, 52.8 percent of athletes who did not wear headgear suffered concussions, while the rate dropped to 26.9 percent for those athletes that did wear the headgear. (British Journal of Sports Medicine 2008)

There is now also evidence that shows that while intentionally heading of a soccer ball may not cause a concussion, the repetition of heading a ball may lead to concussion-like damage of brain cells. Researchers at Albert Einstein College of Medicine believe that the threshold for having evidence of brain damage appears to be between 1,000 and 1,500 headers per year—only a few headers per day.

That study would make it appear that many competitive soccer players would be at risk for concussion-like brain damage. A reduction in the severity of the blows from headers by headgear could, in theory, change the threshold for number of headers that translates to brain damage. However, there has been no such research done.

While recruiting, Foster said he sees three or more high school players per team wearing variations of the headgear. "In the MIAA (Alma's conference) there are only maybe three other players wearing the headgear, but we have three including Graham," he said.

The use of headgear in soccer may not be fully endorsed by organizations such as the U.S. Soccer Federation or compulsory to wear like shin guards, but soccer—especially youth soccer—may be headed that way.

1. Do you think there is enough evidence to suggest that wearing protective headgear can prevent against concussions? Why or why not?

"YOUTH FOOTBALL TACKLES CONCUSSION ISSUES," BY NICK SMITH, FROM *CRONKITE NEWS*, APRIL 28, 2015

Brian Brooks still remembers the first time he watched his son sustain a head injury playing tackle football. The hit left 10-year-old Carson down on the field, injured – and Brian with a parent's worst nightmare.

"Of course, my first impulse was to run down to the field immediately," Brian said. "It was very hard the first time that happened, watching my kid lay there."

When Carson eventually came off the field, Brian had a decision to make. Years ago, Carson might have missed no time at all, with his coaches eager to rush him back onto the field. But the world of football has changed over the last decade. Head injuries and their long-term ramifications have overhauled long-held beliefs in the sport, making the decision of how long to sit kids out after an injury difficult for parents.

"There were still games remaining in the season," Brian said. "We ended up erring on the side of caution and having him miss at least two full games."

Head injuries in collegiate and professional football have come under intense scrutiny the last few years, and attention has trickled down to the youngest levels of the sport. Many argue youth tackle football has the biggest responsibility of all, as the heads and bodies of young players are still forming.

"The younger brain is more vulnerable to concussion," said Dr. David Dodick, director of the Mayo Clinic concussion program in Phoenix. "Simply because our brain is made up of billions of wires, most of which are insulated. And it takes awhile to lay down that insulation on all of those wires. A lesser degree of trauma, of blunt force, would produce a concussion in a younger person and it takes longer for them to recover."

Last May, Dodick attended the Healthy Kids and Safe Sports Concussion Summit at the White House, where President Barack Obama spoke. On his way home, Dodick thought about the lack of research when it came to youth sports and concussions. Once back in Phoenix, he reached out to the most influential youth league, Pop Warner.

"I felt like while we were studying concussion in collegiate and professional sports," Dodick said. "There wasn't much going on in terms of youth sports. So I felt it was time to reach out to Pop Warner to determine what their concussion policy was, what their sideline protocol was, how their athletes were cared for after a concussion."

Pop Warner immediately responded to Dodick, and, after several meetings, a partnership was formed between the youth league and the Mayo Clinic. It allows the Mayo Clinic to continue to research tools to diagnose head injuries that have been validated at a professional and collegiate level but not yet at a youth one. Pop Warner players are now also baseline tested before the season begins, testing players' vision, balance and cognitive skills so medical professionals can spot a head injury quickly during the season.

"Baseline testing should happen every single year," Dodick said. "It gives us a sense of how their brain is functioning at their baseline. So if they are concussed we'll be able to at least judge them compared to their baseline and we'll know when they get back to their baseline level of functioning."

In 2012, Pop Warner became the first youth football organization to limit the amount of contact a team could have during practice. Players are no longer permitted to participate in full-speed tackling drills when lined up farther than three yards apart.

"Pop Warner was really ahead of the curve," said Mike Funkhouser, vice president of Superstition Pop Warner. "A good method of curbing some of the concussions came from a national limit on contact in practice. They limited the amount of contact to a third of the weekly practice time."

The new partnership allows Pop Warner to make even more improvements in dealing with head injuries. With the help of Dodick and the Mayo Clinic, a return-to-play protocol has been instituted. Injured players are now evaluated by a cognitive specialist, balance expert and neurologist before there is any decision made about when they can return to the field. The Mayo Clinic sees children as young as 8 as part of the program.

"If a player is injured on a weekend, they call a hotline and we get them in on Monday," Dodick said. "The last thing we want is for them never to be evaluated, their symptoms go away, they feel back to normal, then they go back to play the next weekend and they get reinjured. Because that could be devastating. Not only could it be fatal in rare instances but it could lead to symptoms that persist for weeks, months or years. I've seen plenty of that."

The national focus on concussions has made parents of young football players more aware of the dangers of the sport. Brian remembers the hesitation on his part when Carson, the youngest of three brothers, first asked if he could play tackle football. Even for a father of three, the idea of his 7-year-old throwing on pads gave him pause.

"Absolutely there was hesitation," Brian said. "And I'm not a squeamish guy."

But not everyone feels the same. One obstacle doctors have to deal with is parents who want to rush their children back to action. Dodick received multiple concussions playing youth hockey and has been asked by parents why he won't give approval for their child to return to play since he suffered no long-term repercussions from head injuries. Other parents will cite athletes who played collision sports and ended up with no long-term effects from concussions.

"I still think there's a general lack of understanding of the implications of concussions," Dodick said. "You can understand why they're saying that. But that's kind of like saying, 'I know lots of people who smoke who never get lung cancer. Can I condone smoking?' No, of course no ... I also can't tell you if when children are concussed, how many are going to develop prolonged concussion syndrome that's going to affect their ability to perform in sports as well as academically."

The partnership appears to have had a positive effect on young athletes. Now 14, Carson Brooks is playing in Superstition Pop Warner, after playing several years in other organizations. He suffered a second head injury while playing in Pop Warner, and his father noticed a marked difference in the way his injury was treated the second time.

"With the second injury, it was more than just one EMT looking at him," Brian said. "With the Mayo Clinic being involved, you're going to have a more educated set of eyes watching him. I actually mentioned to the coach how much more regimented their concussion program was."

The biggest difference Brian noticed with Carson's injury and within the league itself is a culture shift in which coaches, parents and players acknowledge safety as the primary focus.

"It's clearly about the safety of the athlete," Brian said. "I think they're creating a culture where it's not cool to say, 'Oh just suck it up and get back in there.' Instead it's about nurturing these players to make sure they're healthy. I think that's a great thing."

1. Do you think the culture of sport is changing in the face of such high-profile injuries in athletes? Why or why not?

BIBLIOGRAPHY

Bachynski, Kathleen. "Are Parents Morally Obligated to Forbid Their Kids From Playing Football?" *The Conversation*, June 2, 2015. https://theconversation.com/are-parents-morally-obligated-to-forbid-their-kids-from-playing-football-39764.

Bachynski, Kathleen and Daniel S. Goldberg. "Facing the Concussion Risks of Youth Football." *The Philadelphia Media Network*, September 26, 2014. http://www.philly.com/philly/blogs/public_health/Facing-the-concussion-risks-of-youth-football.html.

Carson, Jeff and Andrew Bennie. "Sports Coaches Need to Be Educated About Concussion to Keep Players Safe on the Field." *The Conversation*, August 1, 2016. https://theconversation.com/sports-coaches-need-to-be-educated-about-concussion-to-keep-players-safe-on-the-field-61975.

Collins, Donald and Lindsey Barton Straus. "Youth and High School Sports Concussion Cases: Do they Show The Limits of Litigation in Making Sports Safer?" momsTeam. http://www.momsteam.com/concussion-class-action-lawsuits-may-show-limits-of-litigation-as-tool-to-make-high-school-and-youth-sports-safer.

"The Concussion Treatment and Care Tools Act of 2015." The US Senate, January 29, 2015. https://www.congress.gov/bill/114th-congress/senate-bill/307.

ESPN.com News Services. "Obama Elevates Concussion Talk." ESPN.com, May 29, 2014. http://espn.go.com/espn/story/_/id/11001328/president-barack-obama-calls-more-research-youth-concussions.

Ferguson, Blane. "From Cheerleading to MMA, Chance for Concussion is Hard to Eliminate." *Cronkite News*, April 28, 2015. http://cronkitenewsonline.com/2015/04/from-cheerleading-to-mma-chance-for-concussion-is-hard-to-eliminate.

Gregory, Andrew. "Testimony of Andrew Gregory, M.D. Before the House Subcommittee on Oversight and Investigation." US House of Representatives, May 13, 2016. https://energycommerce.house.gov/hearings-and-votes/hearings/concussions-youth-sports-evaluating-prevention-and-research.

Janz, Kelli. "Testimony for Public Hearing 'Concussions in Youth Sports: Evaluating Prevention and Research." The US House of Representatives, May 13, 2016. https://energy-commerce.house.gov/hearings-and-votes/hearings/concussions-youth-sports-evaluating-prevention-and-research.

Moyers, Bill. "Pro Football's Unsportsmanlike Conduct." *Common Dreams*, September 17, 2013. http://www.commondreams.org/views/2013/09/17/pro-footballs-unsportsmanlike-conduct.

Nader, Ralph. "New Sports Expose: Changes Needed in All Directions." *Common Dreams*, February 26, 2015. http://www.commondreams.org/views/2015/02/26/new-sports-expose-changes-needed-all-directions.

News Now Staff. "Movie as Game-Changer: Opinions Vary on How 'Concussion' May or May Not Affect the NFL." *PT in Motion News*, December 28, 2015. http://www.apta.org/PTinMotion/News/2015/12/28/ConcussionMovieReaction.

Nowels, Michael. "Barrow Concussion Network Built to Protect Arizona High School Athletes." *Cronkite News*, April 28, 2015. http://cronkitenewsonline.com/2015/04/barrow-concussion-network-built-to-protect-arizona-high-school-athletes/.

Obama, Barack. "Remarks by the President at the Healthy Kid and Safe Sports Concussion Summit." The White House, May 29, 2014. https://www.whitehouse.gov/the-press-office/2014/05/29/remarks-president-healthy-kids-and-safe-sports-concussion-summit.

O'Keefe, Michael. "With NFL Accepting CTE Link, Lawyer for Retired Players Urges Appeals Court to Toss Out Concussion Settlement," *New York Daily News*, March 15, 2016. http://www.nydailynews.com/sports/football/lawyer-court-toss-nfl-concussion-settlement-article-1.2565563.

Ottman, Haley. "Addressing the Long-Term Impact of Concussion in Living Patients." The University of Michigan Health System, June 20, 2016. http://labblog.uofmhealth.org/rounds/addressing-long-term-impact-of-concussion-living-patients.

Parcel, Bill. "Committee Hears Testimony on Pascrell's Youth Sports Concussion Act." The US House of Representatives, May 24, 2016. https://pascrell.house.gov/media-center/press-releases/committee-hears-testimony-on-pascrells-youth-sports-concussion-act.

"Parent and Athlete Concussion Information Sheet." Centers for Disease Control, Heads Up Program, 2016. http://www.cdc.gov/headsup.

Peick, Sean. "Special Report: Combating Concussions in High School Sports." *Cronkite News*, May 6, 2013. http://cronkitenewsonline.com/2013/05/with-law-other-initiatives-arizona-combats-concussions-in-prep-sports.

Pennington, Bill. "A New Way to Care for Young Brains." *New York Times*, May 6, 2013. http://www.nytimes.com/2013/05/06/sports/concussion-fears-lead-to-growth-in-specialized-clinics-for-young-athletes.html.

Peter, Josh. "Packers Players from Super Bowl I Fight to Hang onto Winning Memories," USA Today, Feb. 3, 2016. http://www.usatoday.com/story/sports/nfl/2016/02/03/super-bowl-i-green-bay-packers-vince-lombardi/79756542.

Rudnik, Jakub. "Soccer Concussions Stress Value of Headgear." The Redline Project, November 27, 2013. http://redlineproject.org/sportsconcussionsrudnik.php.

Sahler, Christopher S. and Brian D. Greenwald. "Traumatic Brain Injury in Sports: A Review." *Rehabilitation Research and Practice*, July 9, 2012. http://www.ncbi.nlm.nih.gov/pubmed/22848836.

Schwarz, Alan. "N.F.L.-Backed Youth Program Says It Reduced Concussions. The Data Disagrees." *New York Times*, July 27, 2016. http://www.nytimes.com/2016/07/28/sports/football/nfl-concussions-youth-program-heads-up-football.html.

Sellers, Steven. "Where Is Sports Concussion Litigation Headed?" *Class Action Litigation Report*, February 18, 2016. http://www.bna.com/sports-concussion-litigation-n57982067520.

Smith, Nick. "Youth Football Tackles Concussion Issues." *Cronkite News*, April 28, 2015. http://cronkitenewsonline.com/2015/04/youth-football-tackles-concussion-issues.

"Sports-Related Concussions and Traumatic Brain Injuries: Research Roundup." Journalists Resource, October 22, 2014. http://journalistsresource.org/studies/society/public-health/sports-related-concussions-head-injuries-what-does-research-say.

Stewart, William. "Concussion: Horror of Sports-Related Brain Damage is Only Now Emerging." *The Conversation*, February 5, 2016. https://theconversation.com/concussion-horror-of-sports-related-brain-damage-is-only-now-emerging-54139.

Thompson, Dennis. "Americans Growing More Concerned About Head Injuries in Football," *The Harris Poll*, Dec. 21, 2015. http://www.theharrispoll.com/sports/Football-Injuries.html.

Upton, Fred. "Opening Statement of the Honorable Fred Upton Subcommittee on Oversight and Investigations Hearing on 'Concussions in Youth Sports: Evaluating Prevention and Research." The US House of Representatives, May 13, 2016. http://docs.house.gov/meetings/IF/IF02/20160513/104914/HHRG-114-IF02-MState-U000031-20160513.pdf.

Ventresca, Matt. "Concussions Aren't Only a Medical Issue." *The Conversation*, January 16, 2015. https://theconversation.com/concussions-arent-only-a-medical-issue-35304.

Zegel, Karen Kinzle. "Testimony for Public Hearing 'Concussions in Youth Sports: Evaluating Prevention and Research." The US House of Representatives, May 13, 2016. https://energy-commerce.house.gov/hearings-and-votes/hearings/concus-sions-youth-sports-evaluating-prevention-and-research.

CHAPTER NOTES

CHAPTER 1: WHAT THE EXPERTS SAY

EXCERPT FROM "TRAUMATIC BRAIN INJURY IN SPORTS: A REVIEW," BY CHRISTOPHER S. SAHLER AND BRIAN D. GREENWALD

1. M. Faul, L. Xu, M. M. Wald, and V. G. Coronado, *Traumatic Brain Injury in the United States: Emergency Department Visits, Hospitalizations, and Deaths*, Centers for Disease Control and Prevention, National Center for Injury Prevention and Control, Atlanta, Ga, USA, 2010.
2. J. Gilchrist, K. E. Thomas, L. Xu, L. C. McGuire, and V. G. Coronado, "Nonfatal sports and recreation related traumatic brain injuries among children and adolescents treated in emergency departments in the United States, 2001–2009," *Morbidity and Mortality Weekly Report*, vol. 60, no. 39, pp. 1337–1342, 2011.
3. Centers for Disease Control and Prevention (CDC), "Sports-related recurrent brain injuries — United States," *Morbidity and Mortality Weekly Report*, vol. 46, no. 10, pp. 224–227, 1997.
4. K. M. Guskiewicz, M. McCrea, S. W. Marshall et al., "Cumulative effects associated with recurrent concussion in collegiate football players: the NCAA concussion study," *Journal of the American Medical Association*, vol. 290, no. 19, pp. 2549–2555, 2003.
5. R. C. Cantu and R. Voy, "Second impact syndrome: a risk in any contact sport," *Physician and Sportsmedicine*, vol. 23, no. 6, pp. 27–34, 1995.
6. P. R. McCrory and S. F. Berkovic, "Second impact syndrome," *Neurology*, vol. 50, no. 3, pp. 677–683, 1998.
7. B. D. Jordan, N. R. Relkin, L. D. Ravdin, A. R. Jacobs, A. Bennett, and S. Gandy, "Apolipoprotein E 4 associated with chronic traumatic brain injury in boxing," *Journal of the American Medical Association*, vol. 278, no. 2, pp. 136–140, 1997.
8. M. W. Collins, S. H. Grindel, M. R. Lovell et al., "Relationship between concussion and neuropsychological performance in college football players," *Journal of the American Medical Association*, vol. 282, no. 10, pp. 964–970, 1999.
9. E. J. T. Matser, A. G. Kessels, M. D. Lezak, B. D. Jordan, and J. Troost, "Neuropsychological impairment in amateur soccer players," *Journal of the American Medical Association*, vol. 282, no. 10, pp. 971–973, 1999.

10. L. de Beaumont, M. Lassonde, S. Leclerc, and H. Théoret, "Long-term and cumulative effects of sports concussion on motor cortex inhibition," *Neurosurgery*, vol. 61, no. 2, pp. 329–336, 2007.

11. L. de Beaumont, H. Thoret, D. Mongeon et al., "Brain function decline in healthy retired athletes who sustained their last sports concussion in early adulthood," *Brain*, vol. 132, part 3, pp. 695–708, 2009.

12. K. M. Guskiewicz, S. W. Marshall, J. Bailes et al., "Association between recurrent concussion and late-life cognitive impairment in retired professional football players," *Neurosurgery*, vol. 57, no. 4, pp. 719–726, 2005.

13. M. W. Collins, M. R. Lovell, G. L. Iverson et al., "Cumulative effects of concussion in high school athletes," *Neurosurgery*, vol. 51, no. 5, pp. 1175–1181, 2002.

14. B. E. Leininger, S. E. Gramling, A. D. Farrell, J. S. Kreutzer, and E. A. Peck III, "Neuropsychological deficits in symptomatic minor head injury patients after concussion and mild concussion," *Journal of Neurology Neurosurgery and Psychiatry*, vol. 53, no. 4, pp. 293–296, 1990.

15. M. R. Lovell, M. W. Collins, G. L. Iverson et al., "Recovery from mild concussion in high school athletes," *Journal of Neurosurgery*, vol. 98, no. 2, pp. 296–301, 2003.

16. P. R. McCrory, M. Ariens, and S. F. Berkovic, "The nature and duration of acute concussive symptoms in Australian football," *Clinical Journal of Sport Medicine*, vol. 10, no. 4, pp. 235–238, 2000.

17. B. I. Omalu, R. L. Hamilton, M. I. Kamboh, S. T. DeKosky, and J. Bailes, "Chronic traumatic encephalopathy (CTE) in a national football league player: case report and emerging medicolegal practice questions," *Journal of Forensic Nursing*, vol. 6, no. 1, pp. 40–46, 2010.

18. K. M. Guskiewicz, S. W. Marshall, J. Bailes et al., "Association between recurrent concussion and late-life cognitive impairment in retired professional football players," *Neurosurgery*, vol. 57, no. 4, pp. 719–726, 2005.

19. A. C. McKee, R. C. Cantu, C. J. Nowinski et al., "Chronic traumatic encephalopathy in athletes: progressive tauopathy after repetitive head injury," *Journal of Neuropathology and Experimental Neurology*, vol. 68, no. 7, pp. 709–735, 2009.

20. H. Martland, "Punch drunk," *Journal of the American Medical Association*, vol. 91, no. 15, pp. 1103–1107, 1928.

21. J. Register-Mihalik, K. M. Guskiewicz, J. D. Mann, and E. W. Shields, "The effects of headache on clinical measures of neurocognitive function," *Clinical Journal of Sport Medicine*, vol. 17, no. 4, pp. 282–288, 2007.
22. D. A. Bruce, A. Alavi, L. Bilaniuk, C. Dolinskas, W. Obrist, and B. Uzzell, "Diffuse cerebral swelling following head injuries in children: the syndrome of malignant brain edema," *Journal of Neurosurgery*, vol. 54, no. 2, pp. 170–178, 1981.
23. J. W. McDonald and M. V. Johnston, "Physiological and pathophysiological roles of excitatory amino acids during central nervous system development," *Brain Research Reviews*, vol. 15, no. 1, pp. 41–70, 1990.
24. American Academy of Neurology, "Practice parameter: the management of concussion in sports (summary statement): report of the Quality Standards Subcommittee," *Neurology*, vol. 48, no. 3, pp. 581–585, 1997.
25. Centers for Disease Control and Prevention (CDC), *Heads up: Brain Injury in Your Practice*, Centers for Disease Control and Prevention, National Center for Injury Prevention and Control, Atlanta, Ga, USA, 2007, http://www.cdc.gov/concussion/headsup/pdf/Facts_for_Physicians_booklet-a.pdf.
26. E. Finkelstein, P. Corso, and T. Miller, *The Incidence and Economic Burden of Injuries in the United States*, Oxford University Press, New York, NY, USA, 2006.
27. V. G. Coronado, L. C. McGuire, M. Faul, D. Sugerman, and W. Pearson, "The epidemiology and prevention of TBI." In press.
28. "Nonfatal traumatic brain injuries related to sports and recreation activities among persons aged ≤19 Years—United States, 2001–2009," *Morbidity and Mortality Weekly Report*, vol. 60, no. 39, pp. 1337–1342, 2011.
29. M. Mitka, "Reports of concussions from youth sports rise along with awareness of the problem," *Journal of the American Medical Association*, vol. 304, no. 16, pp. 1775–1776, 2010.
30. L. M. Gessel, S. K. Fields, C. L. Collins, R. W. Dick, and R. D. Comstock, "Concussions among United States high school and collegiate athletes," *Journal of Athletic Training*, vol. 42, no. 4, pp. 495–503, 2007.
31. V. D. Seefeldt and M. E. Ewing, Youth Sports in America: An Overview, 2, no.11, *President's council on Physical Fitness and Sports Research Digest*, 1997.
32. J. C. Goodman, "Pathologic changes in mild head injury," *Seminars in Neurology*, vol. 14, no. 1, pp. 19–24, 1994.

33. R. M. Chestnut and L. F. Marshall, "Management of severe head injury," in *Neurological and Neurosurgical Intensive Care*, A. H. Ropper, Ed., pp. 203–246, Raven Press, New York, NY, USA, 3rd edition, 1993.

34. J. T. Povlishock and D. I. Katz, "Update of neuropathology and neurological recovery after traumatic brain injury," *Journal of Head Trauma Rehabilitation*, vol. 20, no. 1, pp. 76–94, 2005.

35. R. L. Hayes and C. E. Dixon, "Neurochemical changes in mild head injury," *Seminars in Neurology*, vol. 14, no. 1, pp. 25–31, 1994.

36. J. P. Kelly and J. H. Rosenberg, "Diagnosis and management of concussion in sports," Neurology, vol. 48, no. 3, pp. 575–580, 1997.

37. K. M. Guskiewicz, M. McCrea, S. W. Marshall et al., "Cumulative effects associated with recurrent concussion in collegiate football players: the NCAA concussion study," *Journal of the American Medical Association*, vol. 290, no. 19, pp. 2549–2555, 2003.

38. M. Lovell, M. Collins, and J. Bradley, "Return to play following sports-related concussion," *Clinics in Sports Medicine*, vol. 23, no. 3, pp. 421–441, 2004.

39. M. W. Collins, M. Field, M. R. Lovell et al., "Relationship between postconcussion headache and neuropsychological test performance in high school athletes," *American Journal of Sports Medicine*, vol. 31, no. 2, pp. 168–173, 2003.

40. M. W. Collins, S. H. Grindel, M. R. Lovell et al., "Relationship between concussion and neuropsychological performance in college football players," *Journal of the American Medical Association*, vol. 282, no. 10, pp. 964–970, 1999.

41. M. McCrea, K. M. Guskiewicz, S. W. Marshall et al., "Acute effects and recovery time following concussion in collegiate football players: the NCAA concussion study," *Journal of the American Medical Association*, vol. 290, no. 19, pp. 2556–2563, 2003.

42. M. McCrea, T. Hammeke, G. Olsen, P. Leo, and K. Guskiewicz, "Unreported concussion in high school football players: implications for prevention," *Clinical Journal of Sport Medicine*, vol. 14, no. 1, pp. 13–17, 2004.

43. J. T. Eckner and J. S. Kutcher, "Concussion symptom scales and sideline assessment tools: a critical literature update," *Current Sports Medicine Reports*, vol. 9, no. 1, pp. 8–15, 2010.

44. K. Sarmiento, J. Mitchko, C. Klein, and S. Wong, "Evaluation of the centers for disease control and prevention's concussion

initiative for high school coaches: 'heads up: concussion in high school sports'," *Journal of School Health*, vol. 80, no. 3, pp. 112–118, 2010.

45. S. P. Chrisman, M. A. Schiff, and F. P. Rivara, "Physician concussion knowledge and the effect of mailing the CDC's "Heads Up" toolkit," *Clinical Pediatrics*, vol. 50, no. 11, pp. 1031–1039, 2011.

46. R. J. Echemendia, M. Putukian, R. S. Mackin, L. Julian, and N. Shoss, "Neuropsychological test performance prior to and following sports-related mild traumatic brain injury," *Clinical Journal of Sport Medicine*, vol. 11, no. 1, pp. 23–31, 2001.

47. P. McCrory, W. Meeuwisse, K. Johnston et al., "Consensus statement on concussion in sport 3rd international conference on concussion in sport held in Zurich, November 2008," *Clinical Journal of Sport Medicine*, vol. 19, no. 3, pp. 185–200, 2009.

48. J. Bleiberg and D. Warden, "Duration of cognitive impairment after sports concussion," *Neurosurgery*, vol. 56, no. 5, p. E1166, 2005.

49. D. A. van Kampen, M. R. Lovell, J. E. Pardini, M. W. Collins, and F. H. Fu, "The "value added" of neurocognitive testing after sports-related concussion," *American Journal of Sports Medicine*, vol. 34, no. 10, pp. 1630–1635, 2006.

50. V. C. Fazio, M. R. Lovell, J. E. Pardini, and M. W. Collins, "The relation between post concussion symptoms and neurocognitive performance in concussed athletes," *NeuroRehabilitation*, vol. 22, no. 3, pp. 207–216, 2007.

51. S. H. Grindel, M. R. Lovell, and M. W. Collins, "The assessment of sport-related concussion: the evidence behind neuropsychological testing and management," *Clinical Journal of Sport Medicine*, vol. 11, no. 3, pp. 134–143, 2001.

52. I. G. Stiell, G. A. Wells, R. D. McKnight et al., "Canadian C-spine rule study for alert and stable trauma patients: II. Study objectives and methodology," *Canadian Journal of Emergency Medicine*, vol. 4, no. 3, pp. 185–193, 2002.

53. I. G. Stiell, C. M. Clement, B. H. Rowe et al., "Comparison of the Canadian CT head rule and the New Orleans criteria in patients with minor head injury," *Journal of the American Medical Association*, vol. 294, no. 12, pp. 1511–1518, 2005.

54. M. Smits, D. W. J. Dippel, G. G. de Haan et al., "External validation of the Canadian CT head rule and the New Orleans criteria for CT scanning in patients with minor head injury,"

Journal of the American Medical Association, vol. 294, no. 12, pp. 1519–1525, 2005.

55. T. K. Len, J. P. Neary, G. J. G. Asmundson, D. G. Goodman, B. Bjornson, and Y. N. Bhambhani, "Cerebrovascular reactivity impairment following sport-induced concussion," *Medicine & Science in Sports & Exercise*, vol. 43, no. 12, pp. 2241–2248, 2011.

56. R. C. Cantu, "Second impact syndrome," *Clinical Journal of Sport Medicine*, vol. 17, pp. 37–44, 1998.

57. P. McCrory, K. Johnston, W. Meeuwisse et al., "Summary and agreement statement of the 2nd International Conference on Concussion in Sport, Prague 2004," *British Journal of Sports Medicine*, vol. 39, no. 4, pp. 196–204, 2005.

58. R. L. Saunders and R. E. Harbaugh, "The second impact in catastrophic contact-sports head trauma," *Journal of the American Medical Association*, vol. 252, no. 4, pp. 538–539, 1984.

59. L. Longhi, K. E. Saatman, S. Fujimoto et al., "Temporal window of vulnerability to repetitive experimental concussive brain injury," *Neurosurgery*, vol. 56, no. 2, pp. 364–374, 2005.

60. E. J. Pellman, M. R. Lovell, D. C. Viano, and I. R. Casson, "Concussion in professional football: recovery of NFL and high school athletes assessed by computerized neuropsychological testing—part 12," *Neurosurgery*, vol. 58, no. 2, pp. 263–272, 2006.

61. M. Field, M. W. Collins, M. R. Lovell, and J. Maroon, "Does age play a role in recovery from sports-related concussion? A comparison of high school and collegiate athletes," *Journal of Pediatrics*, vol. 142, no. 5, pp. 546–553, 2003.

62. A. Sim, L. Terryberry-Spohr, and K. R. Wilson, "Prolonged recovery of memory functioning after mild traumatic brain injury in adolescent athletes," *Journal of Neurosurgery*, vol. 108, no. 3, pp. 511–516, 2008.

63. E. J. Pellman, D. C. Viano, I. R. Casson, C. Arfken, and H. Feuer, "Concussion in professional football: players returning to the same game—part 7," *Neurosurgery*, vol. 56, no. 1, pp. 79–90, 2005.

64. M. E. Lenaerts and J. R. Couch, "Posttraumatic headache," *Current Treatment Options in Neurology*, vol. 6, no. 6, pp. 507–517, 2004.

65. G. L. Iverson, M. Gaetz, M. R. Lovell, and M. W. Collins, "Cumulative effects of concussion in amateur athletes," *Brain Injury*, vol. 18, no. 5, pp. 433–443, 2004.

66. M. Critchley, "Medical aspects of boxing, particularly from a neurological standpoint," *British Medical Journal*, vol. 1, no. 5015, pp. 357–362, 1957.

67. J. M. Powell, J. V. Ferraro, S. S. Dikmen, N. R. Temkin, and K. R. Bell, "Accuracy of mild traumatic brain injury diagnosis," *Archives of Physical Medicine and Rehabilitation*, vol. 89, no. 8, pp. 1550–1555, 2008.
68. F. J. Genuardi and W. D. King, "Inappropriate discharge instructions for youth athletes hospitalized for concussion," Pediatrics, vol. 95, no. 2, pp. 216–218, 1995.
69. R. Roos, "Guidelines for managing concussion in sports: a persistent headache," *Physician and Sportsmedicine*, vol. 24, no. 10, pp. 67–74, 1996.
70. E. S. Gurdjian, V. R. Hodgson, W. G. Hardy, L. M. Patrick, and H. R. Lissner, "Evaluation of the protective characteristics of helmets in sports," *The Journal of trauma*, vol. 4, pp. 309–324, 1964.
71. B. Hagel and W. Meeuwisse, "Risk compensation: a 'side effect' of sport injury prevention?" *Clinical Journal of Sport Medicine*, vol. 14, no. 4, pp. 193–196, 2004.
72. B. A. Mueller, P. Cummings, F. P. Rivara, M. A. Brooks, and R. D. Terasaki, "Injuries of the head, face, and neck in relation to ski helmet use," *Epidemiology*, vol. 19, no. 2, pp. 270–276, 2008.
73. T. E. Andersen, A. Arnason , L. Engebretsen, and R. Bahr, "Mechanisms of head injuries in elite football," *British Journal of Sports Medicine*, vol. 38, no. 6, pp. 690–696, 2004.
74. M. Mitka, "Reports of concussions from youth sports rise along with awareness of the problem," *Journal of the American Medical Association*, vol. 304, no. 16, pp. 1775–1776, 2010.

GLOSSARY

catastrophic Something that involves sudden and tragic damage.

chronic traumatic encephalopathy (CTE) A degenerative disease found post-mortem in people who have sustained repeated blows to their heads.

compensate To give something in order to make up for some loss.

concussion A brain injury often caused by a heavy blow to the head.

debate A formal argument where opposing sides are presented.

generation To produce or inspire something new.

lingering Something that seems to last much longer than it should.

litigious Being prone to suing others in a court of law.

minimizing Making something smaller or less important.

neurologist A doctor who treats the nervous system.

outcomes The various ways events turn out.

sequelae Conditions that are the consequence of a previous injury or condition.

standardized Something accepted as the norm in comparison to other things.

sustenance The items needed to maintain life, such as food and water.

traumatic brain injury (TBI) A non-degenerative condition that is the result of an injury to the brain and can lead to permanent or temporary impairment.

traumatic encephalopathy syndrome (TES) A brain condition that is associated with repeated blows to the head and which can involve personality changes or behavioral changes, including depression.

FOR MORE INFORMATION

Feudale, Bill. *Personal Foul Unnecessary Roughness: The Ultimate Parents' Guide to Playing Safe Youth Football.* Create Space Publishing, 2015.

Frey, Carol and Feder, Jacob. *Don't Worry My Mom is the Team Doctor: The Complete Guide to Youth Sports Injury and Prevention for Parents, Players and Coaches.* Manhattan Beach, CA: Create Space Publishing, 2014.

Hyman, Mark. *Until it Hurts: America's Obsession with Youth Sports and How it Harms Our Kids.* Boston, MA: Beacon Press, 2010.

King, David and Starbuck, Margot. *Overplayed: A Parent's Guide to Sanity in the World of Youth Sports.* Harrisonburg, VA: Herald Press, 2016.

Kirkendall, Donald. *The Complete Guide to Soccer Fitness and Injury Prevention: A Handbook for Players, Parents and Coaches.* Chapel Hill, NC: University of North Carolina Press, 2007.

Moser, Rosemarie and Pascrell, Bill. *Ahead of the Game: The Parent's Guide to Youth Sports Concussion.* Dartmouth, NH: Dartmouth College Press, 2012.

White, William and Ashare, Alan. *Winning the War Against Concussions in Youth Sports: Brain and Life-Saving Solutions for Preventing and Healing Middle-, High School and College Sports Head Injuries.* Create Space Publishing, 2014.

WEBSITES

Heads Up
www.cdc.gov/concussion/HeadsUp/Training/index.html
This website includes a training session on how to play football safely presented by the Centers for Disease Control.

CRITICAL PERSPECTIVES ON MINORS PLAYING HIGH-CONTACT SPORTS

National Alliance for Youth Sports
www.nays.org
A comprehensive look at youth sports for parents, players, and coaches.

Stop Sports Injuries
www.stopsportsinjuries.org
This site is dedicated to the safety of those involved in youth sports.

INDEX

ABOUT THE EDITOR

John A. Torres is a published author with more than fifty-five books to his credit. He is also an award-winning journalist in Florida who has covered breaking news all over the world, including Africa, Indonesia, India, Italy, Haiti, and Mexico among other countries.

John loves to read, spend time with his family, play fantasy sports, and perform with his band, "The Hemingways."